Over His Head

'Everybody got their bets laid?" Galligan asked. A roar of approval and agreement went up. "Then throw the son of a bitch into the pit! By your emperor's order, throw him in!"

Slocum was swept off his feet and carried along on up-stretched arms. And then he was sailing through the air to and on his back in a seven-foot-deep pit. As he crashed down, a hideous squeaking sounded. Slocum felt wet spots on his back where he had crushed something small and hard. Then he jerked away as a rat bit his arm. Another and another fastened their teeth into him and began gnawing off his flesh. He swung around and sent the rodents flying, but the pit was ankle deep in them.

DON'T MISS THESE
ALL-ACTION WESTERN SERIES
FROM THE BERKLEY PUBLISHING GROUP

JAKE LOGAN

SLOCUM ALONG CORPSE RIVER

J

JOVE BOOKS, NEW YORK

THE BERKLEY PUBLISHING GROUP
Published by the Penguin Group
Penguin Group (USA) Inc.
375 Hudson Street, New York, New York 10014, USA
Penguin Group (Canada), 90 Eglinton Avenue East, Suite 700, Toronto, Ontario M4P 2Y3, Canada
(a division of Pearson Penguin Canada Inc.)
Penguin Books Ltd., 80 Strand, London WC2R 0RL, England
Penguin Group Ireland, 25 St. Stephen's Green, Dublin 2, Ireland (a division of Penguin Books Ltd.)
Penguin Group (Australia), 250 Camberwell Road, Camberwell, Victoria 3124, Australia
(a division of Pearson Australia Group Pty. Ltd.)
Penguin Books India Pvt. Ltd., 11 Community Centre, Panchsheel Park, New Delhi—110 017, India
Penguin Group (NZ), 67 Apollo Drive, Rosedale, Auckland 0632, New Zealand
(a division of Pearson New Zealand Ltd.)
Penguin Books (South Africa) (Pty.) Ltd., 24 Sturdee Avenue, Rosebank, Johannesburg 2196,
South Africa

Penguin Books Ltd., Registered Offices: 80 Strand, London WC2R 0RL, England

This is a work of fiction. Names, characters, places, and incidents either are the product of the author's imagination or are used fictitiously, and any resemblance to actual persons, living or dead, business establishments, events, or locales is entirely coincidental.

SLOCUM ALONG CORPSE RIVER

A Jove Book / published by arrangement with the author

PRINTING HISTORY
Jove edition / September 2011

Copyright © 2011 by Penguin Group (USA) Inc.
Cover illustration by Sergio Giovine.

ISBN: 978-0-515-14990-6

JOVE®
Jove Books are published by The Berkley Publishing Group,
a division of Penguin Group (USA) Inc.,
375 Hudson Street, New York, New York 10014.
JOVE® is a registered trademark of Penguin Group (USA) Inc.
The "J" design is a trademark of Penguin Group (USA) Inc.

PRINTED IN THE UNITED STATES OF AMERICA

10 9 8 7 6 5 4 3 2 1

1

John Slocum knelt beside the raging river gushing down from higher in the Grand Tetons, holding his canteen so that it would fill with the cold, clear water. He jerked back when something heavy smashed against the rocks not a foot away.

He dropped his canteen and went for the Colt Navy slung in his cross-draw holster and had it half out before he realized the body in the river was dead. Standing, he slid his six-shooter back into the holster, reached over, and grabbed the corpse's collar. With a yank, he heaved the body out of the small pool where it had caught, stopping its downstream progress. Slocum rolled the body over. His nose wrinkled at the stench. He had seen worse during the War, but bloated bodies got that way not because they soaked up water but from the noxious gases that formed the longer the body was dead.

Slipping out the thick-bladed knife he carried in a boot sheath, Slocum stabbed out and cut open the belly. He reeled back as the gases billowed up. He had a strong gut, but the smell almost made him lose what little he had eaten at breakfast. It took several thrusts into the mud to clean off his knife before returning it to the sheath. Nose twitching and eyes watering, he bent and searched the body for some way of identifying it.

And truth to tell, a few dollars slipped into a pocket would go a ways toward making his life a mite easier. He had been over in Cheyenne and had a run of bad luck at five-card stud. Although it might have been a couple cowboys working in tandem to cheat him, he thought it more likely that Lady Luck had simply turned her back on him. Slocum had long since learned to walk away while he had a few dollars left, but he hadn't gotten far. The pretty faro dealer whose dress barely restrained her ample charms had beguiled him right out of every nickel he had.

That had been a week earlier. He had ridden due west into the Grand Tetons, staring at the rising mountains and remembering the swell of that faro dealer's breasts with every mile. The early explorers had a wicked sense of humor when they had named these mountains.

He had skirted a dozen ranches, not wanting to remain in Wyoming longer than necessary by running afoul of overly protective cowboys. Years earlier he had spent a winter holed up on the Wyoming plains, one blizzard hardly dying when another came. Trying to escape the fierce weather had entered his mind, but the small cabin where he huddled afforded some protection against the fourteen-foot drifts.

How he had greeted the spring that year was something of a blur, but Slocum vowed never to spend another winter in Wyoming. If he could get across the Grand Tetons and then the Sierra Nevadas, he might reach California before the first real snowfall. He brushed off water from his arms, aware of how cold it felt. He would have to hurry. That first snow might only be weeks away.

Staring at the grotesque, bloated body, he considered what he ought to do. Kicking the body back into the river was the easiest thing. But burial was what he ought to do.

He rubbed his hands against his jeans as he considered what might have happened. The dead man might have been shot. His flesh was in such a bad way that such a wound would never be found—and Slocum wasn't about to look too closely.

The churning river had battered the face and arms to the point where any other cause of death was similarly impossible to determine. For all he knew, the man had died of cholera and had fallen into the water. That thought recommended simply kicking the corpse back to its watery grave and riding on.

Then he saw the second body, turning and rolling in the river. This one was farther out and didn't wash up close to him. From his quick glimpse, that body didn't have a gun belt strapped around its middle either. Slocum put his toe under the body and kicked hard, getting the corpse back into the river. For a moment it hung up on a rock, then part of a sleeve tore off along with gobbets of flesh and the body was caught by the strong current and joined its companion.

He scooped up his canteen and finished filling it. Slocum stared at the canteen a moment, then turned it upside down and let the water drain out. Waiting a few seconds so the water would run clean and free of the detritus from the bodies, he filled the canteen again and slung it over his shoulder by the leather strap. He paused as he looked downstream, thinking he might catch sight of the bodies. The river had swallowed them totally.

Slocum looked up into the pass. Whatever had happened to those men had occurred uphill. He was riding straight into a plague or a gunfight that had sent two men to their fate. From what he remembered, this was the only pass through the Grand Tetons for miles in either direction and another way across to the west would take him a precious week to find.

He touched the ebony handle of his six-shooter, then turned and mounted the paint gelding he had won in a poker game down in Denver. The horse had been his constant companion for better than three weeks now and they got along together well enough.

"Ready to start up the trail? It's mighty steep," Slocum said. The horse turned a big brown eye in his direction, accusing him of vile acts yet to be committed in the name of getting to California. Slocum swung into the saddle and snapped the reins. The paint reluctantly found its way up the steep rocky trail. Slocum patted its neck and settled into the uneven pace, drifting off into a half-dozing state in the warm sunlight. The rushing water to his right was soothing—until a loud thud brought him fully awake. His hand flew to his six-shooter, then he drew rein and stared.

Another body was being smashed against the rocks by the churning river. Then it vanished downstream, disappearing as suddenly as it had appeared. Slocum frowned. One or even two bodies were curious, but a third one? Something was seriously wrong upstream.

Before he could decide whether to turn around and find that other pass through the Grand Tetons, he caught a flash of sunlight off silver ahead. The way the trail meandered about, going away from the river and into rocky areas, sometimes into small stands of trees, and then back out into open straits, he wasn't sure how far ahead the rider was.

He cocked his head to one side and tried to hear the creak of a leather harness or the neighing of a horse. The river drowned out any such noise. Three bodies and one pilgrim not that far ahead on the trail. Slocum's curiosity got the better of him, and he urged the paint upward along the trail. It occurred to him that the rider higher up on the slope would draw any trouble down on his head like lightning, giving Slocum the chance to figure out what was going on.

Three bodies? There could well be more he hadn't seen.

He wanted to make sure his own wasn't added to the flotilla bounding down the river.

Again he caught the reflection of sunlight off what must

be a silver concha decorating a hat. Slocum pushed a little harder to close the distance, aware of the weight of iron at his left hip and the Winchester rubbing against his right knee. Coming out of a small stand of oak mixed with birch and the occasional aspen, he halted again, this time in surprise. Stretching for a quarter mile was an impeccably maintained road that led to a large wooden gate. Someone had gone to considerable trouble to erect both the gate and the rock wall on either side of it, stretching from one canyon wall to the other.

The rider wearing the fancy silver pieces on his hat trotted up to the gate and shouted to a guard stationed inside a tower. Slocum reached back into his saddlebags and drew out his field glasses. The structure was well built and might withstand the attack of an entire company of cavalry. The guard on the tower had loopholes on either side, both with rifles poking out. Whether they had men's shoulders behind the stocks and fingers on the triggers wasn't something Slocum wanted to discover.

The guard stuck his head out of a wider window and called down to the rider.

"You Lasker?"

Slocum couldn't hear the muffled reply, but the guard's head disappeared and less than a minute later a grinding sound of a heavy wooden bar being withdrawn echoed down the canyon and the gate swung open. The rider—Lasker?—trotted through. Putting away his field glasses, Slocum considered the procedure. Pretending to be someone he wasn't seemed a good prescription for getting filled full of holes.

The thought of the bodies going downstream kept coming back to haunt him. The prudent thing to do was turn around and to hell with the time it'd take finding another pass.

"You ride on over to the gate," came the cold command. Slocum glanced over his shoulder at a man on foot with a rifle trained on him. "You got three seconds to start ridin'. One, two, three."

"All right," Slocum said, holding his hands out. "No need to get all itchy in the trigger finger." He used his knees to get his paint pony started toward the gate, once more securely fastened.

He glanced behind him for the gunman, but there was no trace of him. He had faded back into the countryside, telling Slocum more than the gate and wall protected this road. For the life of him, he couldn't imagine what was so valuable that a small army guarded the pass like this.

"Hold up, mister," came the cry from the tower. The rifles in the loopholes swiveled about in a manner that caused Slocum to sit a little straighter. A sharpshooter lurked behind each of the weapons; they weren't just propped up for show.

"What's all this about?" Slocum called.

"Toll road," came the immediate answer. "You got ten dollars, you can pass on through."

"Ten dollars is mighty steep just to ride through a pass nature carved out for nothing." Slocum looked around to see what his chances might be. They didn't look good. There was another guard tower, this one plated in what might be iron originally intended for a locomotive boiler. To shoot through that would take a mountain howitzer. More than a toll road, this was a fortress.

"That's the cost of passage. Take it or leave it."

"How far through the pass?"

"To Thompson."

"That the nearest town?" Slocum shouted. He was getting tired of the long-distance parley.

"Nearest town on the far side of the pass. The ten dollars entitles you to ride on through, spend some time in Top of the World, and get a free drink at the saloon."

"Which saloon?" Slocum asked, stalling for time. He thought he saw a weakness in the wall. Critters had burrowed at the base and others had gnawed the wood. Pulling away three or four of the logs in the palisade would let his horse squeeze through. If hungry animals had begun the job for him, so much the better. From what he could tell, that part of the fence was hidden from both towers because of the way it curved back toward the distant canyon wall.

"Only one. Look, mister, I ain't got all day. You gonna pay or you gonna ride on back down the hill?"

"Ten dollars is mighty steep," Slocum said. "'Less you loaned me that much, there's no way in hell I'm paying the entry price."

"You got that right. There's no way in hell you're gettin' through without payin'. Turn on around and skedaddle."

Slocum started to ask about the bodies caught on the river current, then realized how vulnerable he was. Each rifle barrel had trained on him. One sneeze, one vicious thought, one man bored out of his mind and wanting to see something die, and he would be filled with slugs. It was bad enough knowing he had to expose his back when he rode away.

"See you in hell," he called.

"Not me," laughed the sentry. "I'm on the side of the angels and the emperor!"

Slocum had no idea what that meant but knew he had overstayed his welcome, such as it was.

It felt as if a million bugs crawled up and down his spine as he rode off. He held his breath waiting for a bullet to come sailing his way, but he reached the edge of the improved section of road without mishap. He looked around for the gunman who had gotten the drop on him but saw no trace. Slocum wondered if he had imagined the man until he saw fresh tracks leading away from the road. A quick look in that direction revealed where the guard squatted down, clutching his rifle, partially hidden by scrubby bushes.

Slocum rode on, as if he hadn't spotted the guard. Whatever lay behind the gate—the guard had called it Top of the

World—had to be powerful important for this kind of protecting.

A mile down the road, he turned off and went to the raging river. At this point it tumbled in a quick succession of rapids. He almost expected to see another body, but the sight of fish jumping, trying to get up the river, the spray catching the last light of day and forming rainbows—it all seemed so tranquil, so normal.

He looked over his shoulder in the direction of the gate. Slocum snorted at the idea anyone would pay ten dollars to get through. Who the hell was Lasker that he was passed through without paying? The guard had expected him but obviously hadn't known him, except by name.

He went back over everything he had seen and what had been said.

"Emperor? Top of the World?" He shook his head. Not a bit of it made sense to him, but getting through wasn't going to be all that hard. The guards thought they had to defend against a frontal assault. During the War, Slocum had been a captain in the CSA and had learned a thing or two about tactics. The commanders who squandered their men's lives might win battles, but the cost was always horrendous. Others were craftier and sought new ways to win the battle without decimating their troops.

Slocum had ridden with William Quantrill and had seen the worst that war could offer. Bloodshed for the sake of killing. He rubbed his belly. Quantrill had ordered him gut shot and left for dead after he protested brutality even he could not tolerate. It had taken long months of recovery, and by the time he could walk, much less ride, the War was over and done. That had suited Slocum just fine. Wound or not, he'd had his fill of death.

Slocum found a place to settle down as the sun vanished quickly. He ate some boiled oatmeal and a piece of jerky that didn't have too many worms in it, washed it all down with water from the river, then settled down, hat tipped over his eyes to grab a short nap. He came awake an hour later, alert. He heard drunken singing drifting down from the pass. The gate guards had found themselves a bottle of whiskey and were now serenading the coyotes.

He got up, shook the kinks from his arms and back, then grabbed the reins of his horse and led it back up the path. It took an hour to once again get the gate in sight. Smoke curled up from the far side of the wall, and the aroma of fresh meat roasting reached him. His belly grumbled as his nostrils flared from the savory odor. Rather than go directly to the spot he had identified earlier, he did some scouting.

The sentry who had been posted in the rocks along the trail was nowhere to be seen. From the lack of campfire, cold or hot, Slocum knew the man was stationed only during the daylight hours. During the night, he probably returned to the far side of the gate to chow down with his amigos. Not having to look over his shoulder as he worked on the heavy logs making up the palisade wall suited Slocum just fine.

It was somewhere past midnight when he walked slowly forward, keeping to shadows and staying out of the faint moonlight the best he could. There hadn't been any sign the guards had remained at their posts in the towers, but Slocum took no chances. Even in the dark, the gunmen could kill him easily enough. There was scant cover, and simply filling the air with lead would either kill him or force him to retreat.

Slocum spun and pressed his back against the log wall. He used his knife to pry loose the mud chinks between the sawed tree trunks. Forcing his face into the rough bark-surfaced wall, he looked around the other side. Flickering light gave him an idea where the cooking fire was. He didn't see anyone moving around, but there had to be a few men warming their bones. And although the drunken singing had died down, this was the likeliest spot for it to have originated.

Edging along the wall, Slocum used the knife to test the

integrity of each tree trunk. A slow smile crept onto his lips as his knife sank into soft, decaying wood. The rotted part of the wall he had identified earlier was about perfect for him. Inspection revealed four adjoining tree trunks eaten away at the base where some burrowing mountain critter had dined in high style. Rot had worked its way through other parts of the wall.

Slocum applied himself to digging away with his knife. One section crumbled under his assault. Then another and another. Slocum measured the width with his arms and then eyed his paint. The horse was smallish but sturdy. It had a broad chest, but the three missing logs ought to provide a gap wide enough to lead the horse through.

He immediately found that his horse might scrape through but his saddle and saddlebags stuck out too far. Grunting, Slocum took off the saddle, urged the horse through the wall, then followed with his gear.

He stood stock-still for almost a minute, listening to the night sounds for any hint that the guards had discovered him. Satisfied he was undetected, he saddled his horse and started to lead it away from the wall, in the direction of Top of the World, whatever that might be.

Slocum had taken only a half-dozen strides when he heard the metallic click of a shell being jacked into a rifle receiver. This was quickly followed with three six-shooters being cocked.

He stopped, hoping he was wrong about the sounds. He wasn't.

"You take one more step, mister, and we won't even bother to bury your stinkin', cold, dead body."

2

"I want to kill him," one hidden man whined.

"You know what the emperor said. He wants to pass judgment hisse'f on anybody tryin' to sneak in."

"He just wants to hog the fun of killin' him. Let's do it and not tell him."

A scuffle broke out, giving Slocum a chance to half turn and look around. Two dark figures wrestled around on the ground so he ducked low behind his horse, his hand going for his six-shooter. The response was instant. The air filled with lead.

This spooked his horse, but Slocum hung on for dear life. He was dragged a few yards, got his feet under him, then kicked hard and got onto his horse, bending low in the saddle. He pointed his six-gun at a spot where he had seen a foot-long tongue of orange flame. Three quick shots produced another rifle shot from that guard. Slocum winced as the hot lead hissed past his ear. He sat up in the saddle and was immediately unseated when he crashed into an unseen tree limb hanging low over the road. Tumbling backward, he hit the ground hard and lay there stunned. He stared up

11

and saw the dark limb blocking a patch of stars. Then he had something more blocking his view of the sky.

Four men shoved their six-shooters down at him.

"Go on, mister. The emperor might want to kill you by his own hand, but we could lie. Give us a reason."

"I wanna kill him. Lemme kill him!"

Slocum shook his head and cleared it. The man begging to kill him was a short drink of water, hardly coming to the shoulders of his partners. He might have been a youngster, but Slocum thought he was simply short. He lashed out with his boot and caught the man square on the kneecap. The loud yell of pain was suddenly stifled when Slocum flipped over and swung his leg around like a whip, catching the man behind his injured knee. Slocum's victim toppled backward like a felled tree and lay on the ground making sucking sounds. He'd had the air knocked out of his lungs.

"As much as he deserved that," one gunman said, "I ain't lettin' you do anythin' more."

Slocum brought up his gun and then the night closed in on him as the guard swung his rifle stock and connected hard with an exposed temple.

Pain seemed his constant companion, especially when the loud voices were like driving needles into his brain. Slocum blinked and got a better view after he rubbed his eyes clear. He saw a tall man, thin to the point of emaciation, sitting on a pile of wood in a chair. The man wore a ragged coat that had once been red-and-white-striped but was faded almost to the point of being a uniform gray. Atop the man's head rested a gold circlet canted to one side, almost touching one bushy eyebrow.

"What's he? The village idiot?" Slocum got out, then laughed. It hurt his ribs and caused him to cough loudly. The coughing hid his words.

The man wearing the crown pointed at Slocum and bellowed, "Bow, peasant! Bow before your emperor!"

Strong hands grabbed Slocum and jerked him around so he fell to his knees. A grimy hand on the back of his neck forced his face down into the dirt. Slocum struggled for a moment, then gave up against such overwhelming force. His chance to escape would come later.

"You are an intruder into my empire! You did not pay my tribute but chose to sneak in like a thief in the night."

Slocum grumbled at the self-styled emperor. This earned him a kick to the ribs, and the hand on his neck bowed him over again in forced obeisance.

"Emperor Galligan can be merciful."

The murmur rising from the crowd gathered to see what would happen to Slocum hinted at disapproval.

"But!" Galligan shouted. "But not in this case. Your transgression is too extreme! Lock him up until dawn. Then he goes to the pits!"

Whatever this meant caused a huge cheer from the crowd that soon turned into the repeated chant, "Emperor! Emperor!"

Two guards dragged Slocum to his feet, then kicked them out from under him so they could drag him, toes down, in the dirt. He looked from side to side and then relaxed. Better to let the two owlhoots move him along like this than to be left to the ugly crowd. Not a one of them looked as if he'd be willing to do anything less than shoot Slocum in the gut just to watch him die slowly.

"In there," the man on his right said, dropping him unexpectedly. Slocum barely had time to catch himself before hitting the ground with his face. He levered himself up and saw both men had their six-guns aimed at him. One motioned toward a rusty iron door. Getting to his feet, Slocum went to the door and tried to open it.

"Locked," he said.

"Smart aleck!" The one behind Slocum hit him with the barrel of his pistol. Slocum sensed it coming, ducked, and got only a grazing blow. He tried to grapple with his assailant, but the other gunman crammed his pistol into Slocum's ribs.

Only when Slocum subsided did he pull back with his six-gun and then rap on the door with his pistol butt.

"Open up. We got another one."

"Fer the gangs?" came a drunken voice inside.

"For the pit!"

Slocum had no idea what that meant but both his captors laughed harshly, and when he wrestled the balky door open, so did the corpulent jailer.

The man rubbed his dirty hands together and made obscene sucking noises.

"Ain't had a good 'un fer the pit in a while. The emperor knows how to pick 'em."

"Keep him on ice until dawn."

"What's the betting like?"

"Ain't seen yet. You want to bet?" asked the more attentive of Slocum's guards.

"Ten minutes. He looks like a strong 'un."

"That's gonna be a popular bet."

"Won't matter if I make a dollar or two." The fat man grabbed Slocum by the front of his vest and pulled him into the dim jail. A single coal oil lamp sputtered on a table nearby.

As the two men outside dragged the door shut, leaving Slocum with the jailer, Slocum had to say, "The wick needs trimming."

"Wha—"

The brief instant the jailer's eyes flickered toward the lamp, Slocum swung with all his might. His fist struck square in the middle of the rolls of fat at the man's midriff—and then he thought he'd hit a wood plank. The jailer whoofed and stepped back, slung shot whistling through the air to connect with the side of Slocum's head. The heavy lead-filled bag robbed Slocum of his senses. He felt his legs turn to jelly, and then he simply sat down.

The jailer came over. Slocum watched but could not move as the jailer reared back to kick him in the face. Then he stopped. He dragged Slocum to a cell and threw him inside.

"Don't want to rough you up too much. You wouldn't even last for ten."

"Ten rounds?" Slocum croaked out.

"Ten minutes." The jailer's laugh was as frightening as anything Slocum had encountered since a couple years back when he'd heard the deep rumble of a cattle stampede starting its run toward him.

The jailer returned to his chair and sat heavily. The wood creaked under his bulk but did not yield. Slocum pushed himself up against a cold set of bars. A quick look around told him the outer door may have been rusted but these bars were secure.

"Ain't no way out, mister, 'cept feet first," a bedraggled man in the next cell said. "You're goin' to the pit. I heard 'm say that. Me, I'm bein' sent to the work gangs." He rocked back on the floor of the cell and held up his legs so Slocum could see the shackles already fastened on.

"What's the pit?" Slocum asked.

"You'll find out. You don't look like most of 'em who end up on the gangs—or in the pit."

"How am I supposed to look?"

"Like me. Like them poor bastards in the next cell over. Peddlers. Sodbusters. Men who work for a livin'."

"I work," Slocum said.

"You got the look of a shootist. More like them on the other side of these bars than us."

From the far cell Slocum heard frenzied whispering. The man with the shackles rolled over and exchanged words, then rolled back.

"He's got a point. You might be put here to make us say somethin' we want to keep secret."

"What secret would a peddler like you have?"

"How'd you know I was a peddler? You *are* one of 'em!"

"You talked of peddlers before anyone else locked up here. I figured that was because you sell something."

"Patent medicine. I paid my toll to get through the pass, but they robbed me. They stole all my medicine and took my money. Hell, they even stole my mule. That lop-eared ole mule was my constant companion for close to three years." The man choked up. "They shot him. They shot him for the hell of it, then ate him."

"Reckon my horse is fair game, too," Slocum said. "They'll pay for it." All he heard was a distant guffaw. "Who is that buffoon with the fake crown?"

"Ain't fake. Real gold. Beaten gold. Had precious stones at one time but they kept fallin' out so Galligan gave up tryin' to keep 'em in the crown. Or so I've heard."

"How'd he come to declare himself emperor? Emperor of what?"

"This here town's called Top of the World. It's some kind of private joke. He set hisself up as absolute ruler. Lets through whoever he wants on the road. About chokin' off the town at the other side of the pass."

"Thompson," called a man Slocum couldn't see in the cell beyond the peddler's. "That's its name. Don't know who it's named after, but it's got to be better than this hellhole. I'm slated to be sent out on a work gang, too."

"Leastways, we earn enough on the gang and Galligan will let us go," the peddler said.

Slocum shook his head. He couldn't believe anyone could lie to himself so efficiently. If the self-styled emperor of Top of the World was willing to put them out on chain gangs, there'd be no reason to ever let them go. He had slaves.

"I saw bodies floating down the river on my way up to the toll road gate," Slocum said. "Were they on Galligan's work gang?"

"Don't know nuthin' 'bout that," the peddler said firmly.

"I work hard and earn money and he'll let me be on my way. Hate losin' my mule, but Galligan will let me go. If I work hard enough, long enough."

Slocum had heard similar sentiments in poker games. A little loss turned into a big one, but the gambler always thought that the next hand would make things right. Or the one after that. Victory was always just a bit out of reach, but it could be grasped and all would be right. Before the player knew it, he had dug a hole too deep to ever climb from.

"You ever know anybody working his way off the chain gang?" Slocum asked.

"Hell, no. You get off, you don't stay around Top of the World. You hightail it to Thompson or go east, though there ain't a whole lot in that direction."

"I came that way," Slocum said. He almost mentioned the bodies in the river but held his tongue. The jailer seemed engrossed in doing something on the desk, but Slocum saw the way he had turned enough to overhear everything being said by his prisoners. He was big, but he wasn't stupid. If any of them hatched a plan to escape, he would know all about it.

"What's beyond Thompson?" Slocum asked.

"You kin ride on over to Boise in less 'n a week and be on the coast in two. That's the Pacific coast," the man explained.

"I thought as much," Slocum said dryly. He settled back, winced at the pain in his head, then listened to the chatter between the man in the next cell over and the rest. Telling them they were buying a lie about ever going free was a waste of time, and Slocum wanted to sleep. He had been through too much and needed to save his strength for whatever was in the pit.

He doubted it was going to be as pleasant as working on a chain gang doing whatever Emperor Galligan ordered.

3

Slocum came instantly awake when the jailer shouted and ran his slung shot along the cell bars. He couldn't help himself from reaching to his left hip for the Colt Navy that wasn't there. Slocum sat up.

"Dawn. Time for you to get into the pit." The jailer laughed so hard his belly shook. "On yer feet!"

Slocum stood slowly, waiting to see if the jailer would make the mistake of opening the cell door and afford a chance to dive forward, bowl him over, and get the hell out of the jailhouse. He didn't. He waited for Slocum to stand, pointed to the corner of the small cell, and only then opened the door.

Looking past him, Slocum saw any escape attempt would have been futile. He saw no fewer than three men with six-shooters drawn. From the low murmur, quite a crowd had gathered. Even if he bolted past the jailer, he could never run the gauntlet outside the jail.

"That's a good boy. Don't go gettin' yerself all tuckered out. You want to last at least ten."

"That what you bet?" Slocum asked, leaving the cell when the jailer motioned impatiently.

"I got a hunnerd ridin' on you. Don't go disappointin' me."

"Or what?" Slocum pushed past as the man grumbled.

"You might not last as long as I thought. Could put down a bet for . . . two!"

The jailer laughed, but Slocum saw no humor in it. He had a good idea what to expect. As he went outside, the gathered men shoved him from side to side. Slocum was alert for any chance to grab a six-gun and start firing. He knew he was going to die in the pit. He might as well take some men with him. Maybe the crowd would even cut him down. Better to die in a hail of bullets than whatever Galligan had in store.

The crowd stayed just far enough away to prevent any such grab, even when Slocum saw a man with the familiar ebony-handled Colt Navy stuck in his belt. Slocum knew that he'd die someday—and it was looking as if it was today—but having that owlhoot steal his six-gun rankled more than he cared to admit.

They shoved him along, back to the open square with the pile of logs where Galligan sat on his pathetic throne. He had his gold crown pulled down squarely on his head now. As Slocum watched, the sun poked up over a mountain peak and the first rays caught the crown. If it wasn't pure gold, it was close enough so that it didn't much matter.

"You have offended Emperor Galligan. For that I have sentenced you to the pit." Galligan stood and looked over the assembled crowd. "Is it ready?"

"Never been readier!" cried the man with Slocum's six-shooter thrust into his belt.

"Everybody got their bets laid?" Galligan asked. A roar of approval and agreement went up. "Then throw the son of a bitch into the pit! By your emperor's order, throw him in!"

Slocum was swept off his feet and carried along on up-stretched arms. And then he was sailing through the air to land on his back in a seven-foot-deep pit. As he crashed down, a hideous squeaking sounded. Slocum felt wet spots on his back where he had crushed something small and hard. Then he jerked away as a rat bit his arm. Another and another fastened their teeth into him and began gnawing off his flesh. He swung around and sent the rodents flying, but the pit was ankle deep in them.

"They been starved fer purty near a week, waitin' for yer tender flesh," called down the man with Slocum's pistol. "I got a bet as to which of 'em pukes up your putrid meat first."

Loud catcalls and exchanges circled the pit as Slocum began stamping on the rats. Some of the live ones turned on their wounded or dead brothers. But there were too many famished rats for a few bodies to sate their voracious hunger. Slocum, however, provided an ample meal.

After his first flash of revulsion, he settled down and methodically stamped on the rats, caught them and broke their necks, and otherwise began decimating the population. A hush fell over the crowd. Slocum was bit and bleeding from dozens of wounds, but he was making significant headway toward killing the rats and making the ones he did not destroy cower around the edges of the pit.

"He's beatin' 'em down," came a choked gasp. "How's anybody gonna win the pool if—"

The man didn't get a chance to finish. Standing at the edge of the pit, now towering high over Slocum, stood Emperor Galligan. He pointed at his prisoner and called, "This round is over. Begin round two!"

For a moment there was deathly silence. Even the chittering rats fell silent. Then the crowd roared its approval. Slocum waited to see what new menace would be introduced to the pit. Two men struggled with a box. They kicked the box a couple times, then upended it. A half-dozen mountain rattlers slid from the box into the pit.

For a few seconds, the snakes hissed and slithered about, then saw an incredible amount of food. They started working on the rats Slocum hadn't entirely killed. Seeing the snakes going after the rats and not the human, the crowd began to protest. Slocum wasn't going to wait for round three. That might mean facing a hungry mountain lion. He bent, grabbed a snake by the rattles, and swung it around in a wide arc. The men crowded around the lip of the pit were perplexed. Then Slocum used the rattler like a whip, casting it out toward the owlhoot with his six-shooter thrust into his belt.

The snake's fangs sank deep in the man's hand. He turned, tried to fling off the rattler, lost his balance, and toppled into the pit. Slocum had to step back to let him fall all the way. It took only an instant to whip his pistol from the man's belt. Slocum kicked the son of a bitch in the head, then yanked the downed man's Smith & Wesson from its holster so he'd have more firepower.

Pistol in each hand, Slocum looked up. Both guns were cocked and aimed at Galligan. The two men locked eyes. Galligan's pale blue eyes sparkled in amusement. Slocum's were emerald chips, hard, cold, unyielding.

"Get him out of the pit. He's earned a pardon from me. Emperor Galligan proclaims that this gent is free!"

For a moment, no one moved. Slocum straightened his arm and sighted along the barrel. A single shot would put a slug in Galligan's head.

"I said, get him outta the pit!"

Frantic hands reached down. Slocum tucked the Colt Navy into its holster and kept the captured six-shooter pointed at the emperor. With his free hand, he let a burly man pull him up.

"What about him?" Slocum asked, tipping his head in the direction of the pit but never taking his eyes off Galligan.

"The bets that were on your head are on Zamora's now," Galligan said. A round of grumbling died down as Galligan glared at the men. "Now put down your six-gun. You're a free man. You can go anywhere in Top of the World you want."

Slocum started to ask if he could leave, but he doubted that was in the cards.

Screams from the pit died quickly as the man succumbed to the rattlers' bites or maybe the rats. Slocum wasn't much interested what it was that had caused the sudden silence. The crowd muttered in disgust at the quickness of the death, though a couple hooted and hollered that they had won by betting on less than five minutes between the time of entry to the pit and death.

"You got spunk," Galligan said, looking Slocum over carefully. "I need men like you."

"For the work gangs?"

Galligan looked exasperated and shook his head. The crown dislodged slightly. Up close and in the sun, now up entirely over the mountain peak, the gold circlet looked pathetic once more. He pushed it squarely back on his brow.

"Don't go trying to josh me. Ask any of my boys. I don't have a sense of humor." Galligan glanced around. A full dozen men exchanged looks, shook their heads, and then became frightened when Galligan bellowed, "Tell him I got a *great* sense of humor!"

The men chattered like magpies, each offering up a story showing how funny Galligan could be.

"Shut up," the emperor of Top of the World said, making a dismissive gesture with his hand.

Slocum wondered what would happen if he just gunned down this pretender, then he took a quick look around. Atop three nearby buildings stood riflemen, all attentively watching their leader. He couldn't tell but he thought a couple more snipers were positioned at street level. Their bullets might have to cut through the crowd before reaching him, but Slocum saw that this wouldn't pose a problem for Galligan or his sharpshooters. He might put a bullet in Galligan's forehead, just under the rim of the crown, but he would never get more than a couple paces before he was cut down for such a public service.

"They know their place. And I'd like to offer you a place, too, mister."

Slocum noticed that Galligan never once inquired as to his name. To the emperor, all his subjects were little more than blobs of animated flesh, kowtowing to him. Names were for those who mattered.

"You're offering me a job? Doing what?"

"Guard. I always need men with keen eyes on the wall watching the road. You do a good job, and in a month or two, you might be collecting the tolls." A gasp went up in the men surrounding Galligan. Slocum took this to mean toll collector was a prized job.

"How much would I be allowed to steal before I passed it along to you?"

This honesty about dishonesty startled Galligan. Then he laughed.

"As much as you think you can get away with 'fore I decide to toss you back into the pit. The next time, it won't be rats or snakes."

"The bear," called someone in the gathered crowd. "We ain't had anyone against a bear in a long time."

· Galligan said nothing. He smiled crookedly.

"Reckon you got yourself a guard," Slocum said, thrusting out his hand.

Galligan stared at it as if Slocum had offered him one of the rattlesnakes from the pit. He actually stepped away.

"The emperor don't shake hands. He don't like being touched a'tall," said a man at Galligan's side.

"Well, then let me look around your town and get settled in," Slocum said.

"Be on the wall at noon," the emperor said, stepping away and then walking off haughtily, head high, crown blazing in the morning sun.

Slocum fingered the pistol in his hand, then checked the snipers. He was still in their sights. He waved to them, tucked the S&W into his own belt now, and walked away from the pit. The man's dying gasps were history now. Slocum wondered how they would get the pit cleaned out. Before he reached the main street running through the middle of town, he heard shovels working on the dirt. He turned and saw a half-dozen men, shackles on their ankles, using shovels to fill in the pit. Slocum hesitated, trying to identify any of the men as the ones he had shared the jail with, but he didn't recognize them.

The emperor probably had more than one chain gang hard at work around his town.

That notion didn't set well with Slocum. The War had been fought, the South had lost, and slavery ought to be a thing of the past. In Top of the World it obviously wasn't, no matter what the slaves thought about their fate being working long hours supposedly to earn release. They would never be free again.

The corpses floating down the river told Slocum what he needed to know about how Galligan disposed of unwanted bodies. Those were probably the men he claimed had been freed and had gone on their way.

As he walked slowly down the street, he was amazed at the variety of stores and how the entire town bustled with commerce. If Galligan's heavy hand rested on any of the shopkeepers, it wasn't apparent from a casual inspection.

Slocum stopped in front of the saloon and looked inside. Nothing fancy, but all he wanted was to wet his whistle. His only problem was lack of money. Even if he had his horse and gear, there weren't two nickels to rub together. He turned to go, but the barkeep yelled to him.

"Hey, mister. Wait. Come on in."

Slocum went inside. An upright piano stood in one corner. It was too early in the day for anyone to be banging away on the keys. A billiards table was shoved up against the wall, making it damned hard to play, but he didn't see any cue sticks and there was only one ball on the table. A bar fight or two had probably used up most the equipment necessary for a real game. Two tables were set up for faro and a half-dozen more had poker chips carelessly stacked on them. He and the bartender were the only two in the place.

"You want a drink?" The barkeep was already reaching under the bar for a bottle.

Slocum shook his head. "Can't pay for it."

"This one's on the house. You made me a pile of money this morning. I saw when they drug you in last night that you wasn't a run-of-the-mill drifter and had fight in you."

"What was your bet?"

"That you'd climb out of the pit. I got five hundred to one odds."

Slocum blinked, then had to ask, "How much'd you bet, even with odds like that?"

The barkeep grinned. He had a gold tooth in front just under a split lip that wasn't quite hidden by a thick mustache.

"Ten dollars. They thought I was stupid, but I know a good bet when I see one."

Slocum took the shot of whiskey, then downed it.

"Glad you won."

For a second the barkeep stared, then he laughed.

"You got a sense of humor, too. Can't say that'd much help in a hole filled with rats and rattlers but it surely does go a ways outside."

"What are you going to do with all that money you won?" Thoughts raced through Slocum's head of stealing the money, then getting downhill to the town he'd heard mentioned. Thompson.

"Done spent it. Paid off my mortgage on this here place. It's mine, free and clear. I got a monopoly. The only saloon in town."

"Wise move, business like this." Slocum gestured to the empty saloon. He saw two men step aside as he looked out the door. He started to ask to use the back way, but without a horse he was stuck in town. What he needed was a ticket out of here and the only one he could think of was Galligan. Put a gun to his head, have the emperor order his men back, and Slocum could ride on out untouched.

"Thanks for the drink. It cleared my head some."

"You do look like a man whose destiny is plain enough for everyone to see," the barkeep said.

Slocum left the saloon and looked around. Four more men ducked down alleyways, then peered back to see if he had noticed them. He tried to ignore the lot of them as he walked down the middle of the street, getting the lay of the land and deciding that the fancy hotel at the end of the street was likely where Galligan held court.

Turning suddenly, he ducked down a narrow gap between the bakery and the apothecary shop. He heard rapid bootsteps trying to keep up with him. He got to the rear of the bakery, jumped, and caught a drainpipe to pull himself up to the roof. He flopped down as three men rushed out and looked around. They argued where he might have gone so fast, but none looked up. They split into two groups, one man going east and the other two west. For some reason they never considered that Slocum might have kept going due south. He reared up and tried to see what lay to the south of town, but early morning fog still clung close to the ground.

He dropped back to the alley and returned to the main street. For the moment he had eluded his followers, so he headed directly for the hotel. Before he could go inside, he saw a well-dressed man enter, his top hat brushing the top of the door frame. The man stopped just inside. Slocum saw past to where Galligan stood in the lobby.

Slocum touched the butt of the pistol in his belt, then went to get himself a shield so he could ride on out of town. Galligan wasn't much, but he would have to do.

Barely had his foot touched the first step up to the broad porch around the hotel than movement out of the corner of his eye drew his attention. Two of the men who had been trailing him hurried forward. A quick glance in the other direction showed three more. There had been six and he had only succeeded in losing one. Bad odds.

He looked into the lobby but both Galligan and the fashion plate had vanished.

"Where you goin'?" demanded one of the men.

Slocum smiled crookedly and said, "Reckon the emperor'd want to hear me declare my allegiance to him before I went on duty."

The five men stood in a fanned array around him, saying nothing.

Slocum shrugged. "Another time. I got to get to work."

The one he'd pegged as their leader pointed toward the east.

"Much obliged," Slocum said, turned and walked away, their eyes boring holes in him the entire distance down the road. Even when he left town and walked the quarter mile to the wall, he felt he was being watched. Galligan might have set him free, but he had only traded a cell with iron bars for one with a bit more elbow room. That would have to change. Slocum wasn't the kind to stay locked up for long.

4

"We shoot anybody who doesn't pay?" Slocum asked. The other guard in the iron-clad tower shrugged. Gadsden wasn't much for small talk.

Slocum looked out the loophole and saw he had a good range of fire. He sighted down the rifle barrel and lined the front bead on the spot where he had first stopped on the road to study the wall and the massive gate protecting the toll road. The wall and fortifications had been designed well, except the portion of the wall Slocum had gnawed his way through. He wanted to ask if the hole had been fixed, but knew he wasn't likely to get much of an answer from his new partner.

"Mind if I stretch my legs?"

The man grunted. Slocum didn't know how to interpret that, so he figured it meant it was all right for him to explore. He left the small, stifling hot tower room and saw that a walkway along the wall above the gate afforded a way to the other guardhouse. He looked down the fifteen feet to the ground, then studied the locking mechanism on the gate. From this vantage point he couldn't tell much other than the bar holding the gate shut would resist about any attack that could be mounted. A single rider trying to force his way through had no chance at all.

"You, what are you doing away from your post?"

Slocum looked across the walkway and saw a short, stocky man pointing at him.

"You the boss?"

"As far as scum like you's concerned, yeah. Get on back to work."

"Nobody on the trail to stop," Slocum said. "Mind if I go see how the sentry out along the trail's doing?"

"You stay where you're supposed to. You end up on the other side of the wall and I order 'em to shoot you."

"Unless I can pay the toll?"

This stopped the other man's tirade. He stared at Slocum, eyes going narrow.

"You got money?"

Slocum didn't answer. The sergeant of the guard—that was how Slocum had to think of him—looked around, rubbed his hand over his mouth, then turned back and motioned. This time he wasn't ordering Slocum back into the guardhouse but rather to come across.

Walking carefully on the narrow beam, Slocum went over and saw his guess about the man's height was right. Slocum was tall, about six foot, and the top of the man's head hardly came up to his shoulder.

"You gamble?"

"On duty?" Slocum laughed contemptuously. "What'd Galligan think about anybody doing that?"

"He never comes out here. Hardly anybody moving west. All the travelers come up from Thompson on the other side. They keep tryin' to trade, to get a route for free through Top of the World, but the emperor don't want no part of it. 'Sides, Gadsden back there'd tell Galligan if anything was goin' wrong, that son of a bitch snitch."

"When you've got the best hand, you don't have to bluff," Slocum said. His casual reference to poker had the desired effect.

"Come on inside." The guard ducked as he went into the wooden structure. Slocum had to bend almost double to enter the small door. A quick glance showed this was where the boss stayed. There were two stools and a low table. An empty whiskey bottle stood on the knee-high table along with a worn deck of cards laid out in a solitaire fan.

"Gets mighty lonely out here, doesn't it?" Slocum asked amiably. He moved so that he stood with his back to the small door. The room plunged into near darkness. He looped his toe around the leg of the stool nearest him and sat down. It took a few seconds to position himself so he continued to block the faint light sneaking in through the narrow doorway behind him.

"Gadsden over there"—he pointed back to where Slocum had been stationed—"don't say more than a word or two a week. I swear, he hasn't said two sentences since the day he was born."

"Long as everything's right," Slocum said, sweeping up the cards and shuffling them suggestively.

"Nice to have somebody up on the wall to play cards with," the man said. He licked his lips at the sight of Slocum slowly shuffling.

Slocum scooted a little closer so the table was almost entirely in darkness. He reached into his pocket and clicked down what looked like a silver dollar. It was a mashed bullet he had kept as a memento of not getting killed.

The guard fumbled and pulled out pennies and nickels.

It took Slocum twenty minutes to have the pile of coins in front of him and the bullet tucked back in his pocket so the guard would never know he had been gambling against a worthless slug. Slocum was happy he had won the first hand and pulled in a few of the pennies. There wasn't much to win here, but he took most all of it.

"You cleaned me out," the guard said. "You got to give me a chance to win back some of it."

"Any time. This beats watching an empty trail, jumping at every rabbit and marmot that dashes across."

"I shoot at the marmots. Hate the bastards. One crawled into my bedroll once and bit the hell out of me." He rubbed his crotch.

"Not so many willing to pay to use the toll road," Slocum said.

"Not so many."

"Who gets let through for nothing?"

"Nobody," the man said. He squinted when Slocum slid to the side and let the sunlight fall flush on his face. It was getting late in the afternoon and the sun was threatening to vanish behind a distant peak. "Well, not many. The emperor hires on men from time to time, and they got a special password that gets 'em through the gate without payin'."

"But I reckon they do pay, maybe with their guns?"

"Suppose so. Never thought much on it. They come up, they tell me 'steamboat,' and I wave 'em on through."

"We got to stay till somebody else shows up?"

"I'd go, but I gotta stay. I'm in charge."

"Why don't I go to that saloon in town and get another bottle?" Slocum clicked his thumbnail against the empty bottle. "Seems fair since I was the big winner."

"Couldn't make it there and back 'fore it's time to call it quits," the guard said.

"I'll bring it tomorrow. Be good to have something to do other than play cards."

"I want to win back my money," the guard said. He pursed his lips then waved Slocum away. "Go on, get into town and kick up your heels. But I want the good whiskey, not that piss that Kennard passes off to the regular customers."

Slocum nodded. He stepped out into the cool afternoon air and took a deep breath, then went down the rope ladder, feet once more on solid ground. Starting toward town, he glanced back and saw the guard watching. He waved. The guard ducked back into the wooden tower. When he disappeared, Slocum veered off the road and headed south, exploring the territory with an eye toward getting the hell out from under Emperor Galligan's thumb.

He found a double-rutted road and made better time until it came to an abrupt end. The wind blew across the surface of a large lake, chilling him. After crossing most of Wyoming in the summer heat, it felt more than comfortable. Walking around, he wondered at how the lake was fed, then saw a waterfall that sprang from the side of a large hillside to the west. The usual way of feeding such a lake was from a river, but the river didn't spew from the side of a mountain.

"There might be an artesian well feeding it, too."

Slocum spun at the words, hand going to his six-shooter. He relaxed when he saw a voluptuous redhead seated on a rock looking out across the lake. From the deep scoop neckline and the way it exposed the tops of her snowy breasts, he guessed that she wasn't the schoolmarm.

When she leaned back and lifted her knees, exposing her trim ankles and a considerable amount of calf, he knew she worked as a dancer.

"Like my legs?" she asked. She drew up her skirt, teasing him with inch after inch of new bare skin being exposed. She stopped at mid-thigh. "I'm a dancer at the saloon. No, that's not quite right."

"You've got the legs for it," Slocum said, admiring the sight. The sunset turned her flesh into something golden and her hair positively coppery.

"I'm *the* dancer. And the chanteuse. They tell me I've got quite a set of pipes, but it's the dancing I love most." She stood and made a couple quick turns so her skirt billowed outward, giving Slocum a new vista.

"What do you see out on the lake?" Slocum had to ask.

"Usually not much. Folks in Top of the World don't like coming here. I . . . I wanted to say good-bye to a . . . friend."

Slocum was put on guard by the way she almost started to bawl. She caught herself and brushed away a tear.

"I don't understand," he said. When she pointed, he looked out to the surface of the water. For a moment he didn't understand what he saw floating in the lake. Then the strong current carried the body close enough for him to make out the man's head.

"That's Charlie Olson. Me and him were . . . close."

Slocum watched in gruesome fascination as the body rushed past and vanished at the easternmost side of the lake.

"The river," he said softly, remembering the bodies he had watched rush past.

"Galligan has a spot to the west where he dumps the bodies. The current gets rid of them, so he doesn't have to bury them."

"He has to get rid of that many corpses?" Slocum asked. He read the answer on the woman's face.

"My name's Beatrice," she said.

"John Slocum."

She started to make another spin but slipped and plunged off the rock. Slocum moved like a striking snake and caught her. For a moment, he kept his balance and then lost it as his foot slipped in the sandy lakeshore. The two of them collapsed into a heap, Beatrice sitting on Slocum.

"You kept me from getting hurt."

"Not that," Slocum said. "You'd have fallen into the lake so I kept you from getting wet."

Her bright green eyes fixed on his. A tiny smile crept to her lips and she shook her head.

"You're wrong. I am getting wet."

She bent and kissed Slocum full on the lips. Her weight pressed him down, her breasts rubbing against his chest. He saw no reason to fight the inevitable. She had him pinned. He returned her kiss with the fervor she delivered it.

Somehow Beatrice skinned out of the top of her dress and displayed her nakedness proudly to him as she straddled his waist. She reached down and caught her own nipples and tweaked. Slocum wasn't sure if this, the cold breeze blowing across the lake, or something more turned those rosy nubs into hard pebbles. He crushed her hands down with his own, then got a chance to play with the rubbery nips. She moved her hands on top of his and pulled them down harder. She threw her head back, sending a cascade of bright red hair whipping about like a pennant caught in the wind.

"That feels so good," she said with a deep sigh. She leaned forward and stared down into his eyes, saying nothing more. Her hands left his to run down his chest, to unbuckle his gun belt, to find the buttons on his fly.

Slocum gasped in relief as his hardness was released. She caught it in the circle of her fingers and squeezed gently, rhythmically.

"My, my, you are a big boy, aren't you?"

She rustled her skirts about, lifted her hips, and settled down. Slocum wasn't surprised to find she wore nothing under her frilly skirt. She clung to his manhood, guided it upward, and then let him stroke back and forth a few times in the deep pink canyon hidden under her skirt.

Slocum gulped. The heat, the dampness, it all excited him as much as looking up between her tits to her face now drawn in sexual pleasure.

She repositioned her hips and he sank balls deep into her heated core. Slocum gasped at the sudden rush inward. He forced himself to control his physical reactions. It had been quite a while since he'd had a woman and even longer since he'd been with one as lovely as Beatrice.

She rocked back and forth, her hands now resting palm down on his chest for support. Slocum found himself driven to thrust upward, to sink deeper into her. When he did, she squeezed with strong inner muscles, massaging his hidden length and making him sweat just a bit more.

She groaned in excitement, gripped a double handful of his vest, and began rising and falling faster, setting the pace of their lovemaking. Slocum wanted to do more, but he was pinned beneath her. Truth to tell, she was doing a fine job of arousing him and was obviously getting off on how she moved, the way she twisted from side to side, the tiny practiced twitches she gave.

"You're getting bigger inside me. I didn't think you would. You were already so—" She cried out as Slocum arched his back and drove straight upward, sinking as deeply into her as was possible. All around him he felt the moistness, the heat, and the clinging, clutching sheath of female flesh.

He sank back but could not keep from thrusting upward again. Beatrice began coordinating her own movements with his thrusting until they were both moaning in stark pleasure.

When Slocum was sure he couldn't stand another instant, Beatrice let out a long, loud cry of release. It felt as if a mineshaft had collapsed all around him. And then he exploded like a stick of dynamite. They rammed themselves together again, greedily seeking more, ever more, sensation. And then they were both spent.

Beatrice sank forward. Her cheek rested against Slocum's.

"Been a while since I shaved," Slocum said. "You might find my cheek a bit prickly."

"After that, I don't care," Beatrice whispered in his ear, but she rolled over so Slocum could half turn and face her. Inches apart, they just studied each other, the silence just fine.

Slocum finally asked, "You always celebrate like this when you lose a lover?"

"Charlie?" Beatrice sighed. "He was good, but he wasn't you. This was a way of forgetting him, just for a minute, and how he was murdered by that son of a bitch Galligan."

"I take it you don't like the emperor much."

"You have a cruel sense of humor. Nobody likes him. Nobody, but they all suck up and run around bowing and scraping because he'll send them down the river if they don't."

"If everybody's against him, it wouldn't take much to send him down the river, as you put it." Slocum thought those words were strange but certainly summed up Galligan's control. If the emperor didn't like somebody, he murdered him and tossed the body into the lake so the current would sweep it down the river.

"I know what you're thinking," Beatrice said.

Slocum reached over and toyed with a rubbery nipple.

"You're thinking to jump in the lake—alive—and get the hell out of here. I know a couple people who tried. Galligan's got a guard outside the east gate watching for that. If the guard doesn't shoot you, the river will smash you into the rocks and kill you. Nobody gets out of here alive—without Galligan saying so."

Slocum had wondered why the sentry had been positioned outside the gate. Now he knew. His job was to watch the river for anyone trying to escape, not catch hapless riders in a trap between the gate and the sentry's gun.

"Why's he here? Galligan?"

"He's where he can have complete control over anybody falling into his trap, that's why. He's made himself a rich man extorting tolls from the travelers."

"The road from the east isn't that well traveled," Slocum pointed out.

"The ones who do travel it are willing to pay big money to get on through. The next nearest pass is ten miles away."

"Couriers?"

"A lot of them. And people going to Thompson. That's a goodly sized town on the western side of the pass."

"Does he control the food and other supplies going to Thompson?"

Beatrice shrugged. "Don't see much coming through, which might be why their marshal lets Galligan sit on his damned throne. You've seen it? The throne?"

Slocum nodded. His hand pressed down into warm flesh. He felt her responding again. To his surprise, he was hardening also. It took Beatrice only a few seconds to discover that.

"The people in Thompson might not like having an outlaw haven on their doorstep, but it's not that big a problem for them. They can trade north-south as well as farther to the west."

"Do tell," Slocum said. He grunted as her hand began moving with slow, deliberate motion up and down his stalk. Beatrice snuggled a little closer so he pressed down more firmly on her breasts.

"The outlaws pay Galligan a fortune to hide out here. There's not a whole lot for them to steal here that doesn't belong to him, so they're peaceable enough while in town. But they range throughout western Wyoming and into Idaho and up into Montana. There's not a U.S. marshal in the region that wouldn't love to haul off half the residents of Top of the World for the reward money."

"And what would you like to do?" Slocum asked.

"Right now, I can't think of anything better than this." She tugged him closer still and scooted so she lifted her skirt to reveal a coppery tangle nestled between her thighs. "And later, later, maybe we can get the hell out of here, you and me."

Slocum was amenable to both ideas, but started with the more pleasurable one first.

5

"The son of a bitch cheated you," the guard said. He looked up from the half bottle of whiskey Slocum had put on the low table in the guardhouse and shook his head. "I'll cut his throat for rookin' you like this."

Slocum had bought a half bottle, not wanting to spend all the money he had won off the guard. He had claimed this was all he had and the guard had jumped to the conclusion Slocum had wanted—that the greenhorn was being robbed.

"Don't worry about it. You can have the whiskey. I owe you that much." Slocum touched the spot on his vest and traced the coins there. He still had close to a dollar left. It wasn't much but it was something.

"That's good of you. I'll have to stand you a buck or two for another game."

Slocum kept from smiling. The guard thought he was tapped out and was willing to loan him money for another poker game. Slocum settled down when he realized it might not be anything more than the game making the crushing boredom of standing watch a little easier to take. Slocum

39

looked across the walkway to the guardhouse where he was supposed to stand watch. His partner there muttered to himself but never once said an intelligible word.

"We need to—"

"Hold up," the guard said. He pressed his eye to a loophole and spent enough time looking so that Slocum found another hole to peer through. A half-dozen men rode up. From their look, Slocum identified them immediately as hard cases. The wood wall suddenly seemed a lot less secure if these six opened fire. One of them was festooned with pistols. Slocum caught his breath when he counted eight six-shooters thrust in his belt and dangling from straps.

Slocum and the rest of Quantrill's Raiders had always carried at least that many six-shooters when they invaded a town. A dozen men could sport the firepower of a full company. They would ride through the town shooting at anything that moved. Slocum could usually get off thirty or forty rounds. At the other end of town, they would knock out the cylinders, replace them with fully loaded ones, and then go back through the shocked town, taking their time to pick off any resistance that might have formed.

There usually wasn't much after the first ride through town, but Slocum often had found enough men and sometimes women willing to make a stand for their life and property to justify emptying his six-guns again.

The rider with the other five had the look of a man who didn't much care what he shot. Man, woman, child, it didn't make no never mind to him.

"I know the leader," Slocum said. The rider dressed all in black in the lead rode straight for the gate. Looking down on him, Slocum struggled to put a name to the baby face. The rider didn't look like he was fifteen, but Slocum was sure he was much older. The instant he heard the high-pitched, squeaky voice, he remembered.

"Kid Summers," he said under his breath. Slocum had been in an Abilene saloon when the Kid had decided to get

SLOCUM ALONG CORPSE RIVER   41

roaring drunk. He had stripped off his clothes and jumped to the bar wearing nothing but his boots and gun belt. After he shot the barkeep, Slocum had swung a chair at the Kid's legs and knocked him to the sawdust-covered floor. By then the marshal and four deputies with shotguns had arrived. They took the naked, cussing drunk Kid Summers to jail.

The Kid might have been drunk but he had sworn to kill Slocum.

That had been five years ago, and the kid had been drunk as a lord. Slocum doubted he would remember.

"Got to go talk to 'em. They look like the sort who'd belly up to the bar with Emperor Galligan." The guard left and called down, "What kin I do fer you gents?"

"Let me through," the Kid shouted in his squeaky voice.

"You gotta pay a toll."

"I'm Kid Summers, and I don't pay squat. Galligan asked for me to drop by."

"He give you the, uh, password?"

The Kid exchanged looks with the heavily armed man, then laughed. The sound was like dragging a knife point across slate for Slocum.

"He likes to play games. I don't."

"Can't let you in unless you pay up or give the password."

"We can shoot our way in," the Kid said.

The guard motioned for Slocum to step out and stand by him. Slocum held his rifle, but he watched Kid Summers closely for any sign the outlaw recognized him. The Kid never gave him a second glance.

"Two men?" The Kid laughed. Then his second-in-command tugged at his arm. He had spotted Gadsden in the armored guardhouse as well as the sentry posted out by the river to make sure no one escaped Top of the World. Even with incredible firepower, the gang would be sure to lose a few of their number with their retreat cut off and the wall blocking progress.

"Ain't anything out of the ordinary," the guard said. Slocum heard the tremor in the man's voice. He clutched his rifle a little tighter and began to judge distances and where to send his first bullet. The owlhoot with the eight six-guns would be the first to die, even though Slocum wanted to take out the Kid.

"Steamboat," the Kid said, looking bored. "That what you want to hear, you idiot?"

"Open up for the emperor's guests," the guard said.

Slocum shinnied down the ladder and worked to pull back the heavy locking bar. As he swung the gate open, the Kid crowded through and gave Slocum a long, angry look. Then the other five pushed close behind, and the outlaw moved on. He rode off without another look back. Slocum considered his chances sneaking through the gate and taking out the sentry along the river.

But what good would that do? The sentry didn't have a horse, and it was a long walk to anywhere. He put his back to closing the gate and getting the bar back into place.

"He looks like trouble," Slocum said.

The guard shrugged.

"There's nuthin' but trouble in town. I got a reward on my head," the guard said. Seeing Slocum's look of disbelief, he puffed up and said, "I robbed a train. They want me over in Cheyenne. Real bad."

"Desperado," Slocum said softly. This vague statement settled the growing ire in his boss.

"Damn straight. And don't forget it. I can be every bit as dangerous as . . . as them."

"You know them?" Slocum asked, trying not to sound too anxious.

"I know their kind. They'd as soon shoot you in the back as look at you. The baby-faced one. Their leader." The guard shuddered. "I seen his like come to town more 'n I want to remember."

"Why do you think Galligan is getting them all in like he is?"

"There's been a lot of them the past couple weeks." The guard frowned as he looked at Slocum. "How'd you know that? You only been here a couple days."

Slocum gave some nonsensical answer. It had been a guess. He had seen the gunman ahead of him ride through without paying. Now the Kid Summers gang had arrived. It made sense that Galligan had summoned others.

The rest of the watch crept by like it had been dipped in treacle. Slocum was glad when the four guards from town came to relieve him and the others. He walked into town by himself, wrapped in his own thoughts. By the time he got to the main street, it was already dark. He wasn't too surprised to see gaslights sizzling and casting bright yellow light along the storefronts. For all its remoteness, the town was fairly modern. He doubted there were elevators in the hotel, but other than this, Galligan knew how to live.

The crash of a six-shooter brought Slocum around. He suspected that Galligan knew how to kill, too. The pit was evidence of his sick pleasure, but that could be amusing only so many times before the blood and misery began to pale. Galligan undoubtedly had other pastimes to keep himself amused.

Slocum sauntered along the main street getting the lay of the land. If he hadn't known better, he would have thought this was a law-abiding town. The occasional report from a pistol or the scream of someone getting the shit kicked out of him belied that. Nowhere he looked did he see a lawman. But he did see roving bands of men such as the one that had followed him the day before. He didn't have to be told these were Galligan's equivalent of a police force, only they were answerable to no one but the emperor.

He stopped across the street from the fancy hotel where he had seen Galligan talking with the well-dressed man the day before. The lobby was brightly lit and inviting. A sitting room behind a bay window looked out over most of the main street. A chair with a low table to its side sat there prominently. It was a more fitting throne than the one Galligan used atop the pile of logs.

A single step into the street and Slocum froze. He slowly stepped back and found a bit of shadow to cloak him. Galligan and Beatrice came down the stairs from the hotel's upper floors. They were arm in arm, and she had her head resting on his shoulder. Her coppery hair spilled over and partially obscured his gaudy jacket cut so that he could easily reach the six-gun holstered at his side. Slocum didn't have to hear what Beatrice was saying to know what she suggested. The idiotic grin on Galligan's face told Slocum it was something salacious, something lewd and probably illegal in most other towns.

That Beatrice was sleeping with Galligan wasn't as much a surprise to Slocum as the way she clung to the outlaw's arm the way a drowning woman would hold on to a log to keep from going under. Galligan stopped in the center of the lobby. As if they were dewdrops forming on leaves in the cool morning, three gunmen came from hidden corners of the lobby to stand behind Galligan.

He spoke to them, and they hurried out into the street, each going in a different direction. Whoever Galligan had summoned wasn't obviously in a place known to his henchmen. And Slocum never doubted for an instant that the emperor had sent the trio of gunmen to bring back someone to his court.

Galligan sat in the chair in the window, Beatrice standing obediently behind him. A waiter came up and placed a shot glass and a bottle of whiskey on the table. Galligan waited for Beatrice to pour for him, then downed the drink. He didn't offer her any of the liquor, and she didn't seem surprised at the oversight.

This bottle was for the emperor's palate alone.

Slocum rested his hand on the cold butt of his Colt Navy and considered how easy it would be to fire a single shot. Through glass was a problem. As it broke, the bullet would be deflected. But if he fired fast enough, the plate glass would shatter and leave a clear trajectory for his second and third shots.

He didn't draw. There was too much he didn't understand about Top of the World. If the leader was killed, what would happen? Galligan was no fool. He would take precautions, but how many in the town would welcome his death?

How many wouldn't? Slocum stared at Beatrice, who seemed completely devoted to Galligan. Had her plea at the lake been nothing more than a test to find out where his loyalty lay? If so, Slocum knew he was in a world of trouble should his name come up or if Galligan asked Beatrice.

He slipped along the darkened boardwalk and went to the solitary saloon now overflowing with men who looked nothing like the pictures on their wanted posters. Sidling up to the bar, he ordered a beer. From the nickels he had remaining in his vest pocket, he could order a couple more. Then he would either have to sit and play the gate guard a few more hands of poker or figure another way to earn money. Nothing had been said about him getting paid for his sentry duty on the wall. He had been ordered, and he had gone.

The beer was so bitter that he almost spit it out. But once he had choked it down, the familiar warmth of raw alcohol blazed in his belly and soothed the aches and pains. The barkeep knew how to mix his brews.

After the second one, Slocum decided to call it a night. He still wanted to prowl around the town and try to figure out what Galligan was up to. More than this, he needed a more permanent place to sleep other than the stables with his horse. The stableman had reluctantly allowed him to curl up on some straw but had warned him about not spending a second night there. He might have to be content with taking his bedroll and finding a sheltered spot at the edge of town where he could sleep under the stars. This high up in the mountains it got downright cold at night. If he didn't find a way out of town soon, he would be sleeping in a snowbank.

He set the beer mug down on the bar with a click, turned, and plowed into Kid Summers, knocking the boyish bandido back a couple steps.

"Sorry," Slocum said. "Didn't see you."

"You callin' me short?" The Kid squared off, hands poised over a six-gun holstered at either hip. Slocum had seen only a couple gun slicks who could use either hand equally well, and from what he remembered, the Kid wasn't one of them. All he had to do was pay attention to his right hand. If it twitched, then Slocum drew and fired. At this range he wasn't going to miss.

But he looked over the Kid's shoulder and saw the owl-hoot lugging around the small arsenal and another of the gang. They separated so each could get a good shot at Slocum.

"Let me buy you a drink."

"I know you," the Kid slurred. His eyes widened. "I *know* you!"

Slocum had seen this before. If a man learned something drunk, he could only remember it when he got drunk again. Kid Summers had ridden up sober and hadn't recognized Slocum. Now that he was knee-walking drunk, he remembered their encounter in Abilene.

"You probably didn't recognize me sooner because you still have your clothes on," Slocum said. "You going to dance naked for us anytime soon and show everybody how really short you are?"

The Kid went for his six-shooter, but Slocum had pegged him right. The left hand was slow and awkward so all he had to do was stop the right from reaching the pistol hanging at his side. He stepped forward, reached out, and batted the Kid's hand away so his fingers just brushed the butt of his six-gun. He never got a chance to draw. Slocum's fist ended on the point of the jutting chin, snapping his head back. The Kid's legs buckled and he sat down, stunned.

Slocum recovered his balance, stepped over Kid Summers, and had his Colt out before either of the two outlaws could so much as move for their own six-shooters.

No one said a word. For a moment Slocum was caught like a bug in amber. Quiet. No movement. Then he pushed past the two gunmen and rushed into the street, sucking in a deep breath of the cold mountain air. The haze that had settled on his brain from the beer vanished in a flash. He took a second breath and knew he had avoided leaving bodies behind on the saloon floor.

One of those bodies might have been his if there'd been a third henchman in the saloon.

He walked quickly toward the hotel Galligan had turned into his palace, but a loud cry from behind forced him to stop and turn.

Kid Summers squeaked out his challenge.

"Never knew yer name. I like it that way. They can bury you with just a X on the headstone."

The Kid wobbled, but he was enough in possession of his senses to stand in a half crouch, his hand at his side, ready to draw. Slocum reminded himself that some men learn skills drunk and can't repeat them unless they get drunk again. He suspected the Kid had fought in enough throw-downs drunk to be adept.

"I killed six men. Yer gonna be lucky number seven!"

"You want to die?"

"I ain't gonna die. *You*, you're the one's who's gonna die!"

The Kid twitched, and Slocum went for his six-gun. Slocum was no gunfighter, but he was fast and accurate. He cleared leather and had the hammer drawn back when the report echoed down the street. He stood frozen, his Colt aimed at the slowly collapsing Kid Summers. He turned and covered the two henchmen, who stared in disbelief.

"You killed him. You killed the Kid," muttered the outlaw with the wagonload of six-shooters hanging all over him.

Before Slocum could deny he had fired a shot, he heard the click of boot heels on the boardwalk to his left. A quick glance revealed Galligan, a still-smoking pistol in his hand.

"I killed him. I didn't give orders for him to kill nobody or screw nobody tonight. Till I do, you keep your guns in your holsters and your dicks in your jeans."

Slocum jumped when Galligan fired a second time, dropping the lesser armed member of the Kid's gang. His former gang.

"I didn't like his looks."

"You like mine?" The man with all the weaponry squared off.

"You're new leader. What's your name?"

"Pancho. Pancho Smith."

"Well, well, Mr. Smith, this is your lucky day since my dealings with the former Kid Summers are very lucrative."

Slocum saw how Galligan played the outlaw to win him over. If Smith didn't watch his back, Galligan would put a couple rounds into his spine and never think twice on it.

Beatrice came up behind Galligan and laid her hand on his left shoulder. Her expression was one of pure evil. She looked for all the world like the men who had gathered around the pit the day before, expecting to see someone torn apart by rats or die from snakebite.

For the briefest instant, their eyes met, but Beatrice quickly rested her head on Galligan's shoulder as she whispered more in his ear.

"You gents remember this. Nobody dies in Top of the World unless I order it." He looked significantly at Slocum, then tucked his six-gun away and walked arm in arm back to the hotel with Beatrice.

Slocum saw Smith twitch as he started for a pistol. He wasn't above shooting Galligan in the back after what he'd done, but he settled down, gave Slocum a look of pure hatred, then stalked off. It took all his control for Slocum to keep from calling out that Smith had done the right thing. On the roof of a building across the street, outlined against the rising moon, stood a sniper. Slocum wondered if there were others posted to protect Galligan.

He suspected there were.

He had to find himself a place to sleep for the night. As he passed the open door to the hotel, he saw that Beatrice wouldn't have to worry about finding a bed for herself that night. Galligan herded her up the stairs, his hand on her rump.

Slocum wondered what their bedroom talk was like. He hoped that his name was never mentioned. His quick strides took him to the stable, where he got his gear and finally pitched camp behind a woodpile at the edge of town. Sleep came slowly, and when it did, his dreams were filled with Beatrice laughing at the sounds of dead bodies splashing in the raging river.

Corpse River. That was all he could think to call it. Corpse River.

6

Slocum stirred and then sat up. The sun crept above the distant peak, telling him that he had overslept. The dawn came late in the pass and sunset early up here in the mountains. He stretched, then reached for his six-shooter when he heard a rustling noise in the pine needles a few yards away. He swung around, got his back to the woodpile, and waited.

A flash of red preceded Beatrice creeping from the wooded area. Slocum held his six-gun, wondering if he ought to holster it or just shoot her. She saw him and her face lit up like the sun coming over the mountain.

"John," she said, hurrying forward now that she was sure he had spotted her. "I tried to find you last night."

"Why?"

"You . . . you weren't hurt when Kid Summers called you out?"

"You know I wasn't," he said. "You were at Galligan's elbow when he shot the Kid."

"Why'd he want to shoot it out with you?"

Slocum didn't want to get into the sordid history. He

shrugged and finally said, "A drunk gets his dander up mighty quick. He had the look of being a mean one about him."

"He seemed to know you," she said slowly. Her emerald eyes bored into him. "Did you ride with him?"

"With *him*?" Slocum snorted. "One of us would have been dead a long time before last night if I had."

Beatrice looked worried.

"You sorry he was killed?" Slocum watched her face closely for the reason behind her questions. Something ate away at the woman and he wasn't sure what it was. A nagging idea chewed on him like a rat on a piece of leather that Galligan had put her up to asking these questions.

"What? Him? I didn't know him and he was far too arrogant for my liking." She looked hard at him again. "What's wrong? I wanted to find you last night to . . . to invite you into a more comfortable bed."

"Yours?"

"Yes. What's wrong with that?"

"It'd be a mite crowded, and I'm not used to sharing, especially with someone like Galligan."

"I'm not—"

"I saw you with him."

Beatrice looked angry, then laughed unexpectedly. The sound was bitter.

"I have to," she said. "How many women have you seen in Top of the World?"

"Haven't had a chance to look." He thought on the saloon and didn't remember any pretty waiter girls or hostesses plying their trade.

"There're damned few. I can be a whore or I can prostitute myself with one man. I prefer Galligan to dozens of the scum that drift through town. As long as I keep him happy, he's not likely to put me out to pasture—with a whole herd of horny bulls."

Slocum nodded slowly. There wasn't a whole lot he could

say. Being under the self-styled emperor's protection was preferable to being sold for a quarter a bang in some whorehouse to any gunman who rode through.

"I was with you, John, because I wanted to be."

"Not to find out my plans?"

"I want your plans to be the same as mine—to get out of here."

"More outlaws are coming into town. Do they all meet with Galligan?" Slocum asked.

"They do. There must be a couple dozen cutthroats come to town in the last month."

"Is he recruiting an army?"

"I never thought of it that way, John," she said. "He might be. But why?"

"Tell me about Thompson."

"That's where we have to escape. Out the west gate. It was a small town until a few months ago, and from what I hear from those coming up the pass from town, it's more than doubled in size."

"Why?" Slocum knew that rumors could cause towns to swell in size and then become ghost towns overnight on the basis of rumor alone. Gold? Silver? He had seen his share of boomtowns and wondered if Galligan had heard such rumors and brought in his army to jump a claim or two.

He shook his head. That made no sense. The self-appointed emperor needed to do nothing more than shoot a miner or two in the back to steal a claim. Gathering a small army of gunmen made no sense since he'd have to split his take with them.

Beatrice shrugged her lovely shoulders, looked pensive, and finally said, "Might be something to do with mining. He brought in an engineer or two along with the shootists."

"What else is in Thompson?"

"Escape," she said without hesitation. "There's no way to get back down the pass to the east, the way you came to town."

"There's nothing for a goodly distance," Slocum admitted, but with a couple horses and adequate supplies, it wouldn't matter. "We could go south a week or so and find another pass to the west."

"Thompson," she said firmly, "is our best hope. You don't know Galligan like I do."

"You can say that again," Slocum said dryly. Beatrice shot him an angry look. For a moment he thought the volatile redhead would storm off, but she settled back down, letting her ire cool a mite.

"He'd send men after us. A dozen. More. There's no way you could fight them all off."

"He values you that much?"

"I told you. He doesn't give a hoot and a holler about anyone, and that includes me. But I'm his *possession*. He thinks he owns me, and nobody takes what belongs to the emperor of Top of the World."

"You've thought this out, I see."

"I've had time, and now I get the feeling that there's not much left for me. Whatever he's planning is building steam. Once he devotes himself to it, I'm a distraction—"

"And expendable," Slocum finished for her. He saw the answer in her eyes. When Galligan succeeded in whatever scheme he was brewing, he wouldn't need a dance hall girl anymore. He could afford expensive painted ladies from San Francisco and Denver.

"We've got to work together, John. If we don't, we're both going to die here."

"Galligan wants me alive for some reason. He wouldn't have ventilated the Kid if he didn't have plans."

"He wants to see you."

"He sent you to fetch me?" Slocum looked sharply at her.

"Don't worry. He doesn't know about us. I mean, about . . . us. I made it sound like it was the last thing in the world I wanted to do, finding you and giving you the message."

Slocum knew Galligan was cunning. He stood and looked around for any hint that Beatrice had been followed. Galligan might have sent spies after her to report on what she did once she found him—and if she knew where to find him quickly. Slocum thanked his lucky stars that finding a place to sleep had been so difficult. Beatrice had hunted him down rather than making a beeline to his lair.

"I could use some food, but I reckon getting to hear Galligan's orders is more important."

"We . . . we're partners?" she asked. "In getting out of here?"

"Partners," Slocum said and then he sealed the deal with a long kiss. To hell with anyone Galligan might have sent to report back. Slocum knew he could explain this kiss, if he had to. And if he didn't, he would have learned something important—Galligan had no real interest in Beatrice and was likely to have her thrown to the wolves at any instant.

"Well," she said, stepping back. Her tongue lightly circled her lips and a feral smile lit her face. "You know all the legal terms and how to make things stand up."

"But not in court," he said, laughing. Slocum shoved his Colt Navy into his cross-draw holster and shook off the leaves and pine needles that clung to his clothing. The fragrant pine made him feel a little better about not bathing. Most cowboys didn't bother much, but he found it easier to get rid of the bugs intent on chewing at his hide if he took a bath every week or two.

The pine needles made him smell more respectable in the meantime.

He set out for town after cautioning Beatrice to wait a spell before following. If there was gunplay, she wouldn't get caught up in the middle. He walked down the middle of the main street, alert for any sign of snipers intent on filling him full of lead. The town stirred but hadn't yet come to full life.

He walked to the hotel, where Galligan made his headquarters, and stopped out front of the fancy carved wood doors with the etched glass windows set in them. He considered just storming on in and demanding to see Galligan, but Slocum had a bad feeling about doing that. If Galligan had summoned him, he'd be waiting.

Less than five minutes later, Galligan came out, flanked by four gunmen. Their steely eyes fixed on Slocum. A single gesture from Galligan would have all four slapping leather and firing at Slocum.

"You wanted to see me?"

"You got a mouth on you, Slocum," Galligan said. "You speak when I tell you."

Slocum said nothing. He could provoke Galligan or he could let him get around to telling why an audience had been requested. The emperor had taken the time to learn his name. Slocum worried about such interest.

Slocum snorted at that. Beatrice might have passed along the message but it was hardly a request. Nothing Galligan did was a request. It was always an order. That was what an emperor did—command his subjects.

"We got company on the way."

"Then I'd better get to the gate."

"Hold your damn horses, Slocum. The invasion's comin' from the other direction. From Thompson."

"Invasion?"

"What else do you call it when an army tries to take over your empire?" Galligan laughed at this. "You got a good head on your shoulders, and you look like you can use that hogleg."

"Rifle, too," Slocum allowed. He wasn't telling Galligan anything the man didn't already know.

"You'll need it. Stop the invasion and there's a reward in it. All the booze you can drink and your choice of a whore for the night. That goes for everybody," Galligan added, looking to either side. The four gunmen showed emotion for the first time. Slocum wasn't sure if it was the promise of whiskey, women, or killing that excited them the most.

"Silas here's in charge. You do like he says." Galligan motioned the dourest of the outlaws forward. Slocum tried to place him. He had seen Silas somewhere before, but with the horde of cutthroats the emperor had assembled, it might have been off a wanted poster rather than from a personal run-in.

"I'll mount up and get on over there," Slocum said.

"No need to hunt for your horse." Galligan pointed, using his chin in Indian style. A youngster led five horses down the street. One of them was Slocum's paint. "You men do your job and there'll be liquor flowing like that damned river yonder." Galligan pointed in the general direction of the lake and the raging river draining from it. He waited until Slocum and the other four had mounted before returning to the hotel.

Slocum watched him disappear inside before saying anything.

"What's his hold on this town?" Slocum wondered aloud.

"This." Silas had his six-shooter out of the holster so fast Slocum didn't even see a blur. Slocum wasn't the fastest hand around; there were plenty enough quicker on the draw. But he had never seen a man handle a pistol the way Silas had demonstrated.

"Good enough for me," Slocum said. He didn't add that being fast meant shit unless you were also a good shot, but he had the gut feeling that Silas was as accurate as he was quick.

They rode in silence, Slocum taking in every detail of the road to the western gate. It had been constructed to endure a siege. The wall was close to six feet thick and built of piled stones. Mud had been poured over the rocks to fill in the chinks and give it even more substance. The walkways along the top of the wall allowed two riflemen to pass without doing the dance of the prairie chicken to get past each other. And the gate itself was solid oak, barred with a thick beam secured with iron loops.

"Nobody's getting through that," Slocum said. "Not unless they use a cannon."

"We'll sure give 'em the gate," joked another of the gunmen. Silas frowned and shut him up.

"Get your asses up onto the wall," Silas said. "And don't fall asleep. I see anybody nodding off and I'll cut his throat." He made a wickedly sharp knife appear as if by magic in his left hand. His right loosely held the reins, but Slocum got the feeling Silas was ready to throw down if any of them—especially him—objected to the orders.

Slocum kicked his leg over the horse and dropped lightly to the ground. He tethered the paint, then climbed the crude ladder to the walkway. The two men already pacing back and forth paid him no heed. They remained focused on the broad, well-kept road winding away from the gate.

The road to Thompson was better kept than the one rising to the far gate in the east. Slocum wondered how much the town supplied Top of the World's food. From the condition of the road, he suspected all food and a goodly amount of the guns and ammunition came from Thompson.

That made it all the stranger that Galligan had gathered an army. If the town wanted to cut off his supplies, the emperor would have to fight his way down the side of the mountain. And once in town, other than a one-time looting, what did Galligan gain? Trade was more profitable for everyone concerned.

"There," shouted a lookout perched higher in the rocks to Slocum's left.

Standing on tiptoe Slocum caught sight of a dust cloud moving toward the wall. Rattling chains and struggling mules added to the picture before the heavily armored wagon rounded the last bend and came fully into sight.

Slocum lifted his rifle to his shoulder but did not fire. The range was still great. He had been a sniper during the War and had made longer shots, but he wanted to see what was going on. He had seen a few armored wagons like this in his day, but the driver had never hauled it up a mountainside to use against a fortified gate.

Sporadic gunfire came from around. In the distance those bullets ricocheted off the iron plates hanging on the sides of the wagon.

"Take cover!" He took his own advice and crouched behind a low rock wall as barrels thrust through slits cut in the sides of the iron plating and the men inside opened fire. The slugs tore past him in volley after volley. He chanced a quick look up and caught a bullet through the brim of his hat. Slocum ducked back down as the riflemen inside the armored wagon reloaded and commenced firing again.

"Don't hide, you lily-livered coward!" Silas walked along the wall, oblivious to the bullets tearing past him. He had singled out Slocum for his ire. "Emperor Galligan says to stop 'em. You do that by firin' that rifle in your worthless hands!"

Silas started to kick Slocum to get him into action, but Slocum would have none of that. He drove the butt plate on his rifle smack into Silas's kneecap, sending the gunman reeling. As a new volley from the wagon filled the air, Slocum thought he might have saved Silas's life. He cursed that notion. Better to let him die than to save him, but he wasn't about to let Silas kick like a balky mule.

A quick twist let Slocum see the wagon again. It looked more like a steel porcupine now, sides bristling with rifles protruding. The men inside fired constantly, but the shock of their initial attack faded second by second. Galligan's men got their senses back and started firing from their positions above. The slugs pinged away but now and then Slocum heard a yelp of pain. In spite of the slits in the iron being only slightly larger than the rifle barrels sticking out, some of the intense fire from the wall found its way inside.

Slocum wondered if the slugs would bounce around inside or if the attackers had had the sense to line their iron cage with wood to prevent that.

He turned and pointed his rifle at Silas, who struggled to sit up. He had swung his rifle around to cover Slocum but saw, even with his lightning reflexes, that he was a dead man if he tried to shoot.

"Get into the battle, damn you. Galligan's not payin' you to malinger."

"Galligan's not paying me," growled Slocum, but he chanced another look up to see a hatch opening on the roof of the armored wagon. His reflexes got the better of him. He winged the man poking his head out. The wounded man dropped back into the bed of the wagon.

"More like it," Silas said.

"Let Galligan know," Slocum shot back. Then a new menace drove them both under cover. A Gatling gun opened up from below, sending rock splinters and bits of wood from the gate flying in all directions.

If such blistering fire continued much longer, they would reduce the gate to flinders and be able to drive right on through to Top of the World.

Slocum fired a few times, but the gunners working the Gatling were protected by sloping iron plates. He might wound one or the other but that wouldn't stop the fire directed against the gate.

"Give 'em everything you can," Slocum yelled. He worried that Silas would take the chance to shoot him in the back. Then he was over the wall, dangling for a split second and dropping to the hard-packed road in front of the gate.

Not a foot above his head ripped the flood of bullets from the Gatling gun. Slocum considered shooting at the two men operating it again, his angle better on the ground than it had been on the roof. Whoever had planned the attack counted on all enemy fire coming from above, not the ground. Only a couple of the gun ports on the rolling fort had been cut low enough for the riflemen inside to shoot at anyone on foot. Slocum dropped to his belly and scooted forward in the dust.

His approach caused the mules to kick up their hooves. Already frightened from the pitched gun battle, the team began backing up. Whoever drove the wagon had not set a brake and had relied on the mules in harness to hold the wagon in place. As the animals shied, the wagon began rolling backward.

Slocum slid out his knife from the top of his boot and hacked away at the harnesses. The nearest mules kicked and tried to flee from him, causing even more consternation in the team. He severed one trace and then another before working up to the thickest leather straps in the harness. He found that his plan worked with only half the yoke cut.

"We're rollin' back downhill! We're gonna die if this damned thing goes over a ledge!"

From inside came frantic sounds, then two hatches popped open as the men tried to abandon their now dubious safety inside. Silas and the rest of Galligan's sharpshooters picked them off as they struggled to get away from the wagon, now rolling faster and dragging a few of the mules still held in harness.

The noise deafened Slocum. The mules, the gunfire, the men's anguished cries as they were wounded or killed created such confusion that he feared for his own life. Silas would surely gun him down if he came into his sights. But more immediate danger forced Slocum to hang on to the wagon tongue as the ponderous bulk gathered speed and rolled back downhill.

If he let loose, if he stopped being dragged underneath the wagon, he would be killed instantly.

Slocum let out a shriek as the armored wagon bounced at the verge of the road and then plunged down into a ravine— with him still clinging to the undercarriage.

7

Slocum tried to let loose of the wagon tongue when the war wagon began to topple, but his coat sleeve caught on a nail. Dragged down the hillside, Slocum gritted his teeth and jerked as hard as he could to get free. His coat finally yielded and a large piece of cloth continued tumbling down the hill, still attached to the wagon. Slocum rolled a few yards and finally grabbed a rock to stop his fall.

He twisted about and looked at the bottom of the ravine, where the armored wagon had come to a halt amid a cloud of dust. Slocum started to climb back up the hillside to the road, where sporadic gunfire continued, signaling that Galligan's men were taking potshots at the survivors of the wagon who had bailed out. But he saw an arm flailing about through the top of the armor. Somebody had survived the fall.

Slocum released his grip, dug in his boot heels, and controlled his slide down the rest of the way to the bottom. He slid his six-shooter from its holster as he approached.

"You try poking a gun out and I'll shoot you dead," Slocum called.

"I surrender. Don't kill me." A head followed the words. The man held his hands above his head as he wiggled from the destroyed wagon. The iron plates had buckled, turning the once invincible rolling fortress into a coffin.

As the man came out, Slocum caught the glint of sunlight off a deputy's badge.

"Anybody left inside?" Slocum asked.

"Dead. Two are dead. What about the marshal and the rest?"

Slocum glanced up to the road and saw Silas herding three men toward the gate.

"Captured's my guess."

"You gonna kill me?"

"Why were you trying to get through the gate?"

"What are you, touched in the head?" The deputy spat blood and a tooth.

"Tell me."

"Galligan's got to be stopped, that's why we was attackin'." He spat again, this time only blood. "Got me something busted up inside. A rib, maybe." He winced as he moved. From the way his face had gone as white as bleached muslin, Slocum knew the deputy wasn't faking his injuries.

"Sit down in the shade."

"Why? That make it easier to kill me?"

"I'm not going to shoot you," Slocum said. "Tell me why you attacked with this . . . thing." Words ran from him as he tried to corral them to describe the ironclad wagon.

"Marshal had the idea. Tried to dig Galligan out a couple times, but that damned defensive wall of his was too strong. A handful of men with rifles held us off, so he decided that we oughta build this." The deputy gasped as new pain wracked him. "We couldn't get a cannon so the marshal rustled up a Gatling gun."

"You'd have made it through the gate if it hadn't been for the mules."

The deputy looked at him with dull eyes. Slocum wondered if the lawman realized why the mules had balked and sent the wagon tumbling over the brink. Slocum made sure his knife was securely back in the sheath at his boot top. He had stopped the attack almost singlehandedly and was feeling that he had made a big mistake.

"Reckon so. You gonna call them boys up on the road? Looks like they're huntin' me."

"Stay in the shade," Slocum said. "If I leave you, can you keep from dying?"

"You're not takin' me prisoner?"

Slocum didn't bother telling the deputy he was as much a prisoner as the marshal and the others Silas held at gunpoint.

"I'll tell them nobody survived the fall. If they come to check, can you hide?"

"Considerin' what'll happen if I don't, yeah, reckon I can. Why are you doin' this for me?"

Slocum motioned the deputy to silence and turned, facing up the steep hillside where Silas stood with his rifle tucked against his shoulder.

"You find anything, Slocum?"

"Dead men. Nobody else," Slocum called back.

"Git your ass up here then. You got a bad habit of malingerin'."

"Don't shoot me while I'm climbing," Slocum said. Silas lowered the rifle and turned to bellow at somebody out of Slocum's field of vision. Slocum began climbing. From behind he heard the deputy call out to him.

"Thanks, mister. I won't forget this."

Slocum dug in his toes and made steady progress up the hill and finally tumbled to the road, only to find himself staring down the barrel of Silas's rifle.

"Oughta cut you down," Silas said.

"What'd Galligan say about that?" Slocum watched Silas's face. Playing poker with him would be a chore. Only a small tic at the corner of his left eye betrayed any emotion, but the way the outlaw relaxed just a mite told Slocum he was safe. For now.

"He's got plans for you."

"Yeah," Slocum said. He saw a small knot of prisoners surrounded by Galligan's men. "How many did you catch?"

"Three. One's the marshal down in Thompson. The emperor's gonna enjoy playin' his games with him. The other two are deputies and don't count as much."

Slocum trudged ahead of Silas, aware of the rifle aimed at his spine. He passed the marshal and the two lawmen who'd been with him inside the armored wagon. They all looked the worse for the attack. The marshal held his right arm in a way that Slocum knew meant broken bones. The other two men leaned on each other to walk.

The gate creaked open, bits of it falling to the ground.

"Shot the hell out of your gate, leastways for a while," the marshal said.

Silas said nothing but went to the lawman and clubbed him. He waited for the marshal to get his feet back under him before hitting him again.

"Git up." Silas pointed the rifle at the marshal. Slocum saw Silas's finger turn white with tension on the trigger but held his tongue. This wasn't his fight. He looked around and saw the guards on the wall all watching the drama unwind. They were silent but the expectant look on their faces told Slocum they wanted Silas to kill his prisoner.

The marshal struggled to his feet and joined his two deputies.

Slocum fell back, thinking this might be a chance to get the hell away from Top of the World, but Silas wouldn't have any of it. He motioned with the rifle for Slocum to mount and ride at point. Slocum led the way into town, Silas and several of Galligan's men following with the prisoners.

Galligan came from the hotel, Beatrice at his side. She

looked more rumpled than she had before Slocum left for duty on the wall. It didn't take much of an imagination to guess what she and the emperor had been up to.

"Silas's got some prisoners," Slocum called out to Galligan. "Be here with them in a minute or two."

"I hear the cheers," Galligan said, nodding. The townspeople were turning out to lend their voices to rousing cries of victory. Galligan stared hard at Slocum. "Why'd you let any of 'em live?"

"Not my call. Silas was in charge."

"Might be he has plans for 'em," Galligan said. He glanced at Beatrice, who grinned from ear to ear in support of the idea. "Boredom's 'bout the worst thing that can happen in a town like this. But you know all about that. You findin' any more rattlesnake whips, Slocum?"

"Just snakes," he said.

Galligan turned angry, then laughed.

"You got grit in your gizzard, Slocum, I'll give you that. Or maybe you don't care if you join them Thompson bastards in a new pit?"

Galligan baited him, and Slocum knew it. He was more interested in Beatrice's reaction. There might have been a flash of fear as Galligan outlined his plans, or maybe it was something else. Slocum couldn't tell if the redhead feared for him or her own life. Galligan would dump her in a pit filled with hungry rats if he thought she had cheated on him with Slocum.

"There's the conquering hero now. Come on over, Silas." Galligan gestured expansively to his lieutenant. "How many of them varmints have you brought me?"

"Got three, Emperor, but this one's special." Silas slid his boot from his stirrup cup and kicked at the marshal, sending him stumbling forward.

The marshal glared at Galligan but said nothing.

"You're new, aren't you? You must not have known that I paid off Marshal Comstock to let me be."

"You're choking off commerce to Thompson," the marshal said.

"What name do I put on your gravestone?" Galligan asked.

"Hank Menniger's the name," the lawman said. "And you'll never write my name on a tombstone."

"You're right, Marshal Menniger. I wouldn't do that because I wouldn't take the time or spend the money for a gravestone. You'll be buried in an unmarked grave. How do you like that?"

Slocum saw how much effort Menniger put into not retorting or even trying to rip out Galligan's throat with his bare hands. Galligan wanted a reaction to feed his own arrogance and give the slowly assembling citizens of Top of the World a show.

"We need a celebration tonight. We got to show our brave guards we appreciate them. A bonfire tonight!"

For a moment there was deathly silence, then the crowd erupted in cheers. Slocum looked at the faces of the men in the crowd and saw a mixture of fear and anticipation. Galligan's call for a bonfire meant something more than it seemed. Before he could ask anyone what Galligan's idea of a fire was, the emperor barked out his order.

"Slocum, get these prisoners on over to the jailhouse."

Silas and his men formed a circle around Slocum and edged him away. Slocum looked down at the prisoners and pointed toward the edge of town. Menniger and his two men slowly made their way, letting Slocum herd them.

"You keep a good watch over them," Silas said. "Me and the emperor got things to talk over."

Silas's men followed Slocum and the prisoners to the jail. He ushered them inside the small building and almost gagged at the stench.

"Christ, is this a jail or a slaughterhouse?" Menniger cried. Slocum shoved him in when the guards started centering their pistols on the lawman.

"I didn't know it was like this," Slocum said by way of apology. He coughed. "Get the bodies out of that cell and the three of you can stay there."

Menniger had to move the decaying bodies in the nearest cell and stacked them in the second. Only then did Slocum lock him up.

"You keep a sharp eye on 'em, Slocum. Silas said so," said one of Silas's men, who laughed and then backed out into the bright sunlight.

Slocum saw that they had all left, turning him wary. He was supposed to secure the prisoners, but if he showed any inclination to escape—or to aid the lawmen in an escape—he had no doubt he'd find the jaws of a bear trap closing around his neck. Galligan toyed with him. Slocum knew it was only a matter of time before the emperor chose to kill him.

Slocum turned grim at the memory of the bodies floating down the river. Galligan killed so many he didn't bother burying them anymore.

"You get my men some water?" the marshal asked.

"I'll see what I can scare up, but I'm in a pickle myself."

"You're not on this side of the bars," Menniger pointed out.

"Might as well be. Top of the World is one big jail cell, and the only one with a key to get out is Galligan."

The marshal looked hard at Slocum, then nodded.

"About what I figured. Comstock lit out the first chance he got and I was hired in from Salt Lake City. Took the job as marshal without so much as setting foot in the town." Menniger laughed ruefully. "That'll teach me."

"Why were you so intent on rooting out Galligan? If you'd stayed in Thompson, everything would have gone on the way it was."

"With the merchants selling him his supplies at exorbitant prices?" Menniger laughed again, more bitterness than before evident. "Things changed. There was the strike in the hills north of Thompson."

"Gold?"

"Coal," Menniger said. "Right now, that's worth more than gold." He grabbed the bars and shook until they rattled. "This is one piss-poor jail. Wouldn't take much to get out of it."

"Don't reckon most men stay long here," Slocum said, glancing at the stack of bodies in the next cell. Flies buzzed and rats crept closer to check their meal.

"Then, as you said, the whole damned town is one giant prison."

"Why'd a coal mine change things in Thompson?" Slocum asked.

"Railroad's coming through. Thompson supplying coal to the train makes it a potential boomtown."

"The railroad would come through this pass?"

"That's part of the problem. Galligan isn't inclined to give his permission to lay track through the center of his pass, not without controlling the coal mine."

"He wants to keep it all under his thumb," Slocum said. It began to make sense. If Galligan owned the coal mine, he could dictate terms to the railroad. With it going over the pass he commanded with his toll road, Galligan stood to become a wealthy man if he could levy any sort of tax on the railroad.

"You're not one of 'em, are you?" Menniger asked.

"If it wasn't for a fluke, I'd be dead—or in that cell with you."

"You a lawman?"

Slocum's reaction caused the marshal to shake his head.

"Sorry I said that. I can see you're more likely to run from the law than to wear a badge."

Slocum started to tell the marshal about his deputy hiding out but the sound of someone moving around just outside the jailhouse door caused him to bite his tongue. He turned to see one of the gunmen riding with Silas leaning indolently against the wall, ear cocked to overhear anything inside. How much he had already heard didn't bother Slocum so much since it was nothing Silas—and Galligan—didn't already know. But anything more, especially about the deputy, would get him dumped into a pit with something more dangerous than rats or rattlers.

He might even find out the hard way what frightened and thrilled the townspeople about the idea of a bonfire.

Slocum nodded to the marshal, then turned and left without another word. He passed the gunman, who didn't make any effort to follow. The other two were nowhere to be seen, but Slocum didn't have the feeling of anyone watching or following him. Still, he turned and doubled back unexpectedly but did not surprise anyone behind him.

With a nonchalance he didn't feel, he explored town, bypassing the saloon and the whorehouse, hunting for any place Galligan's men might be gathering. If they were getting ready for any concerted attack, they were hidden from his casual scouting. As far as Slocum could tell, nothing unusual stirred up the merchants or the men sitting in the shade along the boardwalks.

Circling behind the hotel where Galligan made his headquarters, Slocum found a spot in the shade of a scrub oak, sat, and watched closely. He saw a guard at the rear door, nodding off and occasionally jerking awake and grabbing for a shotgun that slipped from his fingers. A balcony ran around the second floor, and most of the windows were thrown wide open. Occasional figures passed in and out of sight behind billowing curtains. Slocum tried to count how many men Galligan housed on that second floor.

But the third floor proved most interesting. Slocum saw Galligan come to a window and look out. Freezing, hoping the shade camouflaged him well enough, Slocum waited until the self-proclaimed emperor turned and reached into the room. A tiny squeal echoed to Slocum. Galligan held Beatrice close, then released her.

Slocum caught his breath when he saw Beatrice half fall

out the window, her hands on the sill. From her expression he knew what Galligan did behind her. Clenching his fists did nothing to save Beatrice from the indignity of being taken like an animal in plain sight of anyone in town who might chance to look up.

Then Beatrice sagged and vanished back into the room.

He waited awhile longer, and about the time he had decided nothing more was to be learned, he saw Galligan climb through a window on the second floor, followed by Silas and another of the outlaw's gang.

Galligan and Silas spoke in a voice too low to carry. Slocum made a snap decision and crossed to the corner of the hotel. The guard with the shotgun was sound asleep again. Jumping, Slocum caught at a bit of bric-a-brac just under the balcony and pulled himself up so his head was just under the floor.

"I'll meet with Bannock in a couple days. Let it soak in that I done stopped the attack on Top of the World and now he's got nobody else to do his dirty work."

"You want to give him that long to think about it, Emperor?" Silas put his hand on his six-shooter. "Strike while the iron's hot, I say."

"He needs to send a telegram to the home office and get instructions. He's only a yearling when it comes to the railroad. I need to deal with the old studs."

"If you say so," Silas said.

Slocum's fingers cramped from dangling and forced him to kick about, making too much noise, to get his toes onto a small notch to ease the pressure on his hands.

"What's that?" Silas came over, his boots only inches above Slocum's grasping fingers.

"What does it matter?" Galligan said. "We got to take care of a few details—*you* got to take care of them."

"Anything you want," Silas said. "I'm your man."

"The best hired gun money can buy," Galligan said. Slocum doubted Silas heard the sarcasm in the emperor's words. "Those prisoners over in the jail. They're gonna try to escape, and when they do, they're going to kill him."

Slocum craned his head around to hear better.

"Why bother? I can take him."

"I want the marshal to kill Slocum. You might make it look like Slocum was helping him escape, but Menniger's got to pull the trigger."

"Or make it look like he killed Slocum?"

Galligan laughed heartily.

"I like the way you think, Silas. Go on, kill Slocum your-self."

"But it has to look like Menniger did it," Silas said.

Slocum heard Galligan's laughter and knew he had to get the hell out of town. He swung around to shinny down the support and found himself staring down the double bar-rels of a shotgun.

8

"What're you doin' up there, mister?" The sleepy guard with the shotgun had awakened at the worst possible instant for Slocum.

Slocum didn't answer. Instead he kicked free of the post and crashed down on the guard, both elbows driving down hard into the man's shoulders. He yelped and dropped the shotgun when his arms went numb. Squealing like a stuck pig, the guard tried to fight. Slocum swung his arm around and caught the guard around the neck to drag him onto the boardwalk under the balcony.

"What the hell's goin' on down there?" Galligan sounded pissed off at being disturbed in his scheming.

"Nothing," Slocum grunted out. "Just got a charley horse. Damn thing's killing me!" To the guard he whispered, "I'll kill you if you don't hush up."

Slocum applied even more pressure to his choke hold until the guard went completely limp. Grunting with effort, he dragged the man to a chair, dropped him into it, and then pulled the guard's Stetson down over his eyes, making it appear he was asleep. Scooping up the scattergun, Slocum

propped it beside the chair. He wanted to take it with him
for extra firepower, but the shotgun was likely to be noticed
and the siesta would go unnoticed. For a while.

Stopping at the edge of the walk, he listened hard but
heard nothing above. Galligan and Silas might have gone
back into the hotel. He cursed the idea that they were coming downstairs to see what the ruckus was about. He touched
his six-shooter, then took a deep breath and started walking,
trying not to look back over his shoulder. Not drawing attention was his only way to get back to the jailhouse and
spring the marshal and his two deputies.

He cut down an alley and then broke into a run, only to
dive behind a watering trough when Silas and one of his
gang rode down the street in the direction of the jail.
Slocum considered what to do and couldn't think of anything other than freeing the marshal. Getting out of Top of
the World wasn't going to be easy by himself. He might
have a better chance with three others sporting six-shooters.

Getting out of this trap and to Thompson would be easier
if the marshal rode alongside, too. There wouldn't be questions about how he came into town if the lawman vouched
for him. Then it would be a matter of deciding what to do
about Beatrice.

Slocum walked aimlessly for close to fifteen minutes to
let Silas get wherever he rode. Caution finally got pushed
aside by the need for action. Rounding the corner of a harness shop, he got a good look at the jailhouse. As far as he
could tell, only the solitary owlhoot who had been left
stood guard. He made sure his Colt rode easy in his holster,
then went directly to the man standing outside the door,
smoking a quirley.

The guard looked up. Slocum saw the danger reflected
in the man's eyes. Silas had passed along Galligan's orders.

"What's that?" Slocum asked, looking to his right. The
guard foolishly half turned to see what Slocum meant. One
quick move brought Slocum's six-gun to hand and a power-

ful swing landed the barrel against the guard's temple. He sank straight down as if Slocum had robbed him of his leg bones.

Stepping over the fallen man, Slocum ducked into the jailhouse and immediately froze. A second guard had been posted inside and had a rifle leveled at him. In his haste, Slocum had foolishly walked into a trap.

"This is my lucky day," the man said, grinning to show two missing front teeth. "Silas put up a ten-dollar reward to anybody who caught you."

"Yeah, lucky you," Slocum said. He glanced at the marshal, who looked as if he had bitten into a bitter persimmon. The lawman saw his only chance of escape vanish in a heartbeat and all because Slocum had been too eager.

"Now lookee here," came a lilting voice from outside. "You caught him."

Beatrice leaned against the doorframe and positively leered.

"You're going to be Galligan's favorite tonight for catching him," Beatrice said.

"You think? I ain't never been—" This was all the guard got out before Beatrice stepped into the jailhouse and slugged him with a pistol. The guard let out a loud yelp, lowered his rifle to grab the injured spot Beatrice had caused.

Slocum's draw was swift and his aim accurate. He completed the job Beatrice had started. This time the guard fell facedown and didn't stir. Slocum looked up. Beatrice held the pistol in her hands, ready to fire.

"I took it off the yahoo outside. You club him, too, John?"

"We need to get them out of the cell," Slocum said, going to the cell door. He rattled it, but it was securely locked.

"The one outside must have the keys. This one didn't. I watched and he never showed he had the keys." The marshal looked frantic, and Slocum didn't blame him.

Slocum grabbed the man outside and hauled him into the filthy jail, dropping him next to the other guard. A quick search failed to turn up the keys.

"Look around," he ordered Beatrice. "The keys must be here somewhere."

"I don't see them anywhere, John."

"You can't leave us in here!" Menniger shouted.

"I can force open the door if the keys aren't anywhere to be found."

"Galligan might have them," Beatrice said. "He's got this huge key ring. I never figured out what all of them were for."

Slocum cursed. It made sense that Galligan had the keys. He wasn't a man to let the least bit of power slip from his fingers.

"Get us out!"

"Shut up," Slocum said. "I'll figure out how to spring you."

"Silas is coming. Him and about ten others," Beatrice said, peering around the edge of the door.

Slocum saw that the outlaws weren't riding for the jail but were headed for the western gate. A dozen plans ran though his mind and Slocum discarded all of them as being too dangerous. Then he realized anything he did was going to be dangerous.

"Get out of that dress," Slocum said.

"What?" Beatrice looked from him to the three lawmen and then back. "You can't—"

"Take his clothes. He's about your height." He pointed to the man who had been standing guard outside. "We need to blend in. You can tuck your hair up under the hat."

"We can't just ride out, John. We—"

"Do it."

Beatrice looked hard at him to make sure he wasn't joshing her, then took a deep breath and began shucking off her dress. Slocum turned and stood facing the marshal and his two deputies, who craned their necks to get a better look at the stripping.

"You're not leaving' us, are you? You've got to get us out," Menniger said, still straining to see around Slocum and get a look at Beatrice.

"We'll bring back help. If we don't get out, there's no chance in hell for you to," Slocum said.

"You won't forget us?"

Slocum didn't bother answering. He heard the soft hiss of Beatrice's dress being cast aside, then her grunts as she forced herself into the fallen man's jeans. Waiting another few second to give her time, he turned and saw her buttoning the shirt.

He had to smile.

"You fill that out better 'n he ever could," he said.

Beatrice glared at him.

"This better work, John. He's got more lice in his clothes than he does in his hair, and that's saying something." She wiggled, then stopped when she saw how Slocum and the lawmen appreciated the movement. "What about them? When they come to, they'll yell their heads off what's happened."

"Throw us a couple pistols," Menniger said. "We can shoot our way out when somebody with a key finally comes."

"Galligan has it. He won't come over if he thinks there's any chance of that happening." Slocum considered the two guards. "When somebody comes for them, brag about how easy it was to overpower them."

"Their six-shooters. Give us their guns!"

"You'd be dead in a second if they thought you had six-guns," Slocum pointed out.

"If we don't get out of here fast, we're all going to be dead," Beatrice said uneasily.

"Tie them up the best you can," Slocum said, dragging the two guards over to the jail cell. He wished he could open the cell door but there was hardly any rust on the lock. Shooting it open wouldn't work. In his experience a slug only jammed the lock. And shooting fast enough to blow off the lock would bring Galligan's men down on them in a flash.

"Horses around the side of the jail," Beatrice said, coming back. "Silas and his gang are almost out of town now. Hurry, John."

Slocum ignored Menniger's protests and dropped the two guards close enough for the marshal to tie them up. For all he cared, the lawmen could kill the pair. That might be for the best but would ensure immediate execution.

Stepping out into the hot sun, Slocum jumped on the horse that Beatrice had brought around. She had already mounted and shifted uneasily in the saddle.

"What's wrong?" he asked. "You're scooting around like you sat on an anthill."

"Might as well. These damned jeans chafe in all the wrong places."

"I'll have to give you a rubdown when we get out."

"You'd better, John, you'd better!" With that, Beatrice wheeled her horse and trotted off. He watched her for a moment and decided that they had better stay toward the rear of Silas's gang. She was too much a woman to ever wear men's jeans and not give herself away.

"Don't get too close," Slocum warned. "Keep back but not too far."

"I can figure it out," she said, irritated.

Slocum rode to one side of the road and Beatrice to the other so they wouldn't have to eat the dust of Silas's men. Slocum considered staying in the dust to further hide, but no self-respecting cowboy would do that. They would draw more attention than riding the way they did. As if to confirm what he thought, Silas's lieutenant glanced back, saw Slocum, and paid him no attention, turning back to talk with his boss. Slocum heaved a sigh of relief as they neared the gate.

"We'll ride on through with the rest," Slocum said. "Then fall behind once we're out of sight of the guards on the wall."

Beatrice nodded once to show she understood. She pulled up her bandanna to cut some of the dust and held her head down. Even so, she was likely to be noticed from the way the buttons on her shirt strained and her breasts bobbed as she rode. Slocum cut in front of her when Silas stopped and turned to face his men.

"We'll get on down to town. No shootin' once we get there, 'less I tell you. We wait for sundown 'fore we get down to real work." Silas motioned for the gang to ride through, but Slocum caught his breath when he saw Silas stop on the far side of the gate and watch his men come through. The outlaw's sharp eyes took in the details of every single rider.

Slocum had no option but to ride through. If he tried to avoid staying with the rest of the gang, he would stick out like a cross-eyed carpenter's thumb. Slocum followed Beatrice's lead, pulled up his bandanna, and lowered his head.

He got even with Silas. The outlaw sat straighter and started reaching for his six-shooter. Then Beatrice interposed herself between Slocum and Silas. She had lowered her bandanna and put heels to her horse's flanks, bolting ahead to draw Silas's attention. The outlaw ignored Slocum and went after her.

He caught her within a few yards and dragged her off the horse, landing her hard on the road. She got up and began lambasting him for treating her so poorly, promising that Galligan would hear of it.

Slocum trotted on, aware that she had sacrificed her freedom and maybe her life to let him escape. He vowed to do what he could to save her. Killing Silas wouldn't be much of a chore, but Slocum's chance passed as several of the gang rode back to see what caused the ruckus.

Beatrice and Silas argued loudly, with the others joining in. To butt in now, even with six-gun blazing, would be suicidal. Both he and Beatrice would forfeit their lives. Slocum rode a short way down the road, then found a slope his horse could take without breaking a leg. He skidded down the embankment and off the road, heading straight for a tumble of rocks. He vaulted from the saddle and waited, Colt drawn in case Silas came after him.

After five minutes he returned the pistol to his holster. Beatrice had waylaid Silas successfully. What happened to her was likely to be decided by Galligan. Slocum didn't know how fond of having a bed warmer the emperor was. Beatrice was easily the prettiest woman he had seen in the town, but Galligan might have different standards.

Slocum snorted. Hell, he knew Galligan did. Power meant more to him than anything else in Top of the World.

Another ten minutes passed, and Slocum worked his way down a ravine until he came to the ironclad wagon. Taking the deputy into Thompson would afford him some protection from whatever law remained and give him a chance to rally the townspeople against Silas, if that proved necessary.

Slocum thought what it would be like to face Silas and knew he would be cut down in a split second. Never had he seen a gunman with a faster hand. Another man might consider shooting Silas in the back, but that didn't set well with Slocum.

He called, "You still here? You alive, Deputy?" He hadn't expected an answer, but he hoped for some small sound to get him on the right trail. He wasn't disappointed. The scraping sound of a six-gun across leather warned him where the deputy had holed up some distance from the overturned wagon.

Walking slowly, hands out where the deputy could see them, Slocum advanced. He expected a bullet to rip through him at any second, but he was relieved when the deputy poked up from behind a rock, his six-shooter resting on the top.

"You came back. Didn't think you would."

"I finally got out of Galligan's prison," he said. "But Marshal Menniger and two others are still locked up. We need to get a posse and go after them."

"Too late," the deputy grated out. The man's tanned face had gone pale and gaunt. Lifting his six-gun was almost too much of a chore for him. "Take a day to get to Thompson, and after the wagon failed, who in their right mind's gonna go 'gainst Galligan?" His voice trailed off as he slithered back out of sight.

Slocum hurried to the man's side. The deputy was in a bad way, but he had survived this long. He would live until they reached Thompson and a doctor there.

Slocum heaved the deputy up over his shoulder, wondering if there even was a doctor in town. He'd find out—and if there wasn't, at least the deputy could be buried in the town cemetery rather than left out in the hot sun for buzzards and bugs.

He dropped the deputy over his saddle and started downhill to find a place to get back on the road for Thompson.

9

"If I ride another foot like this, I'm gonna die for sure," the deputy gasped out. "Get me down."

"You can't walk, and I don't think you can ride."

"Lemme try," the deputy said.

Slocum helped him slide off the saddle. The deputy came into his arms, and Slocum almost tumbled over with the dead weight, but the lawman stiffened his legs and got himself upright, using both Slocum and the horse to support himself.

"Boost me up. God, my belly's sore."

"As much from not eating as being draped over the saddle," Slocum guessed.

"You got any food? I plumb forgot about eating, it's been so long."

Slocum rummaged through the saddlebags but found nothing. He wished that Beatrice had stolen a better horse, or at least one better provisioned. Then he remembered the woman and wondered how she fared. Silas must have sent her back to Galligan in disgrace. Trying to escape as she had would likely mean her death.

"Nothing. Drink some more water." Slocum waited while the deputy sipped at the canteen and then gagged. The man handed it to Slocum, and he shoved the cork back in to let it dangle from the saddle. As thirsty as he was, he figured the deputy needed it more. If not now, then mighty soon.

"Something's eating you alive. Spit it out," the deputy said.

"A friend helped me escape. She's back there in Top of the World."

"That what Galligan calls his fortress? Fitting."

"You're going to need a big posse to rescue the marshal and the other two."

"So why not rescue your friend at the same time? Looks like we'd be freein' half the town—the other half keepin' them prisoners."

"Cut off the head and the body dies," Slocum said.

"Yeah, but you do that to a snake and it don't die until sundown. That can be a mighty long time to worry about the snake sinkin' its fangs into you."

Slocum boosted the deputy up. It took all the man's strength to hold himself upright but he did.

"Name's Cooley, Gus Cooley."

Slocum was reluctant to let a lawman hear his name. He had more than one wanted poster dogging his footsteps, but a deputy for a small town nestled in the Grand Tetons wasn't likely to have seen any of them. Slocum introduced himself.

"Mighty glad you weren't one of Galligan's men," Cooley said. "Otherwise, I'd be dead right now."

"Wish I could have done more for Menniger, but that cell Galligan has him locked up in is a tight one. And there's only one key."

"And Galligan has it," Cooley guessed. "The man's nothin' if not thorough."

"You might call him that." Slocum walked a few yards,

then had to ask, "You know much about how he runs Top of the World?"

"Only what Menniger had heard from travelers who've paid the toll road fee."

"There any special meaning to him having a bonfire?"

Cooley looked down sharply.

"Why'd you ask? Is he planning one for the marshal?"

"Said he was."

"Damn, we got to get back 'fore that happens. Galligan's notion of a bonfire is to douse a man in kerosene, then make him run a maze of torches. Get too close and the man's burned alive."

"What if the man doesn't set himself on fire?"

"Suppose he's allowed to go free. That'd be something Galligan would claim—and the man's a damned liar. Never heard of anyone getting through without being burned up alive, but I only been in the area for a month or so. Heard other stories of him setting fire to a horse's tail and letting it run till it died of fright." Cooley shook his head. "The man's a dangerous one."

Slocum didn't mention anything about the railroad or how Galligan intended to take over so he could cut himself in on both the freight and the passenger fares as well as selling coal to the railroad.

"I'm going to have to work harder 'n Menniger ever did to whip up enthusiasm for a posse."

"Promise them money," Slocum suggested.

"Ain't got a dime in the kitty. Hell, the marshal's paid me out of his own pocket. There's not a whole lot bein' spent on salaries in Thompson."

"Promise them they can loot Top of the World," Slocum said. "There has to be a passel of money and goods stored there. Galligan can't possibly eat and drink and spend it all by himself."

"The marshal'd never go along with that."

"Tell him after you spring him from the jail. Freedom might go a ways toward softening his outlook."

Cooley laughed, then had to grip the saddle horn with both hands. He began wobbling. He had reached the limits of his endurance. Slocum reached up and pushed him upright. It was a long, slow trip into Thompson.

"You might as well have upped and kilt him," Dr. Radley said, poking the deputy with his finger. Cooley stirred and moaned, but his eyelids hardly flickered.

"He's not going to make it?" Slocum frowned. He had seen men with what seemed to be minor wounds die. He had also seen men with arms and legs blown off who ought to have died on the spot keep breathing—for years. Cooley had been in a bad way, but for the doctor to say he was going to die made thoughts of finding the town's vet flutter through Slocum's mind. Too many times, the vet knew more about medicine and almost always had a better bedside manner.

"Oh, he'll make it. Not so sure 'bout me." The doctor belched loudly. "You took me away from dinner. Tendin' him's cuttin' into my mealtime something fierce."

Slocum drew his Colt Navy and cocked it, pointing it directly at the deputy.

"What the hell're you doin'?" Doc Radley moved faster than Slocum would have thought possible for such an old galoot with a gimpy leg to put himself between the muzzle and his patient. "You been out too long in the sun?"

"It's dinnertime," Slocum said. "Don't want to keep you from your vittles. Besides, the sun's down so there's no way I can get sunstroke."

"Then why're you threatenin' a lawman with a drawn six-shooter? You must have been eatin' locoweed."

Slocum slid his six-gun back into his holster. He had learned what he needed. The doctor might complain about having his mealtime interrupted by a patient, but he was dedicated enough to take a bullet when it looked as if Slocum would have shot Cooley.

"What you want to eat?" Slocum asked. "I'll fetch it for you."

"No need, no need," Radley said, waving a bony hand as if he shooed away flies. "Martha over at the Reserve Café delivers. I sorta like it when she does. She's got a hitch in her gitalong that's mighty nice to watch. And she's not too bad lookin' comin' toward you either."

"Slocum?" Cooley turned and his eyes opened. It took him a few seconds to focus.

"Yeah, here. I brought you to Doc Radley's office."

"That butcher?" Cooley laughed, then coughed. "Glad to see I'm in good hands, Doc."

"You shut yer tater trap and rest, Deputy," the doctor said. "I can't work miracles, and if you tire yourself out, you're gonna croak."

"Slocum," the deputy said, in a stronger voice. "You got to get a posse together. I can't let Galligan keep Marshal Menniger a prisoner."

Truth was, Galligan might have already killed the marshal and his two deputies. Slocum said nothing. Interrupting while Cooley had his say would only tire the man more.

"None of them know me," Slocum pointed out. He wanted no part of leading a posse against the wall protecting Top of the World. Patrolling the catwalk the few times that he had showed him how strong the defenses were. But one thing did gnaw at his conscience. Beatrice had let herself be captured so he could get away. What Galligan might do to her sent cold chills up and down his spine.

Sneaking back into Galligan's little empire wasn't likely to be possible, not after he learned that Slocum had left. Security would be beefed up. Where one or two guards had paced the wall, a dozen might be there now. Galligan might even expect an attack from Thompson.

"What about Silas and his gang?" Slocum asked. "You

said it. Thompson is defenseless without the marshal. It'd
be better for the citizens to defend their own property."

"If him and his gang ain't here now . . ." Cooley's voice
trailed off.

Before Slocum could ask anything more, Doc Radley
pushed him away with surprising strength.

"You git," the doctor ordered. "He needs to sleep. Maybe
time fer him to suck up some of my special medicine." Radley reached over to a table and hefted a pint bottle. He
pulled the cork, and tipped the bottle up against the deputy's
lips, wetting them. A tongue worked across the whiskey.
Cooley sighed and seemed to go into an easy sleep.

Then Radley hiked the bottle to his own lips. The pull he
took lowered the level in the bottle by a good half inch.

"Damned good medicine. Now you git on outta here."

Slocum left and stepped into a cold night breeze. He
pulled his coat a little tighter around himself and considered riding out. His paint was still in a stable back up in the
pass, but leaving it and his gear would be small payment to
save his own hide. Galligan held the entire area in a vise
grip and wasn't likely to let it go.

But Beatrice was still up there. Slocum began walking,
head down and worrying that Galligan might not have
killed her outright. What would he think if he heard that
Galligan had used her as the main attraction in one of his
bonfires? Setting people on fire and letting them run
through the streets for the crowd's amusement turned his
stomach. Slocum could imagine Beatrice's red hair turning to real flame as she ran screaming through Top of the
World.

Slocum realized his hand rested on the ebony butt of his
six-shooter. He relaxed and went to get himself a drink. The
saloon was almost empty, but a small group of well-dressed
men sat in the rear, by the pool table. A half-drained bottle
sat in the middle of their circle as they spoke in low voices.

"You need a shot? Or some beer?"

"Whiskey," Slocum said. The bartender twirled his long, thin, greased mustache tip, then dropped a shot glass on the bar with a loud click and expertly filled it with amber fluid that might actually have been something other than trade whiskey.

"Who're they?" Slocum asked, indicating the men at the back of the saloon.

"You might say they're the town fathers. Leastways, they think of themselves that way. Lou Underwood's the town banker and mayor, the one next to him's owner of the mercantile, the small weaselly guy is the pharmacist, and then there's a representative from the railroad."

"Bannock?" His question startled the barkeep.

"I never saw you in town before, but you know the vice-president of the railroad? You one of them railroad dicks?"

Slocum said nothing as he sipped the whiskey. Let the barkeep think what he wanted. The clatter as somebody slammed the door open caused Slocum to turn. The doctor stomped into the room and ignored Slocum. From the single-minded way he marched over to the men seated at the back of the room, he wasn't likely to see anything.

"You!" bellowed Dr. Radley. "We got problems, and Cooley needs you to help out."

The men at the table exchanged uneasy looks. The one Slocum took to be the banker from the cut of his coat and the expensive gold watch chain bobbing across his belly half stood.

"We're holding a town council meeting."

"There won't be a town left if you do nuthin' more than talk. Cooley needs you to rouse some of yer worthless employees and defend Thompson."

"Doc, we—"

"Now. We got trouble brewin' and you can't jist sit and talk about it."

Slocum finished his whiskey and watched the spectacle of the old doctor berating the city fathers, going around the circle itemizing their failings. Not a one of them liked it but they all sat silent and took it. Radley didn't mince words when he got to the railroad official either. This told Slocum more about the politicians than it did the doctor.

"Git on over to my office. Deputy Cooley'll tell you what's what. He's weak from bein' tortured by that son of a bitch up in the mountains so you got to go to him. If you kin bestir your bones long enough."

Radley shooed the men from the saloon. Slocum started to order a second whiskey when the doctor called out, "You, too, Slocum. He wants you there, too."

Slocum considered getting on his stolen horse and riding away. He had expected to sneak the deputy into town because Silas and his gang might have taken up residence here. Where they had gotten off to, he didn't know. He didn't want to find out either.

"You go on, Doc," he said. "I'll—"

"Now." Doc Radley stamped his foot and crossed his arms, glaring at Slocum.

"You comin', Radley, or do we have to talk to Cooley on our own?"

"He won't bite yer nose off, Mr. Mayor," the doctor growled. He turned to Slocum and said, "Cooley won't chew yer nose off either, Slocum, but I might 'less you come along."

Slocum relinquished. The doctor was going to kick up a fuss until he went along. He trailed the tight knot of politicians who were being herded along by the doctor. This wasn't his fight, but something good might come out of it. If they managed to bring Silas to justice, there might be a way he could trade the outlaw for Beatrice. The notion was hazy and spun about in his head. It didn't sound too likely to work, but he had to think of some plan to rescue her. She had earned his admiration for what she had done decoying the outlaws away from him so he could escape.

He owed the fiery redhead his life.

The town fathers crowded into the doctor's office. Radley waited until he was sure Slocum had pushed his way in, too, standing beside the open door. Cool night air kept the heat of so many bodies standing shoulder to shoulder a bit more tolerable.

"You go on and tell 'em what you done tole me, Cooley," the doctor said.

The deputy was propped up and looking like he had one foot in the grave, but he laid out what had happened and didn't stint on praise for Slocum. Slocum reckoned it was the lawman's way of keeping him in town. Compliments did that for some men, but Slocum thought more of Silas and his lightning draw than he did of being well thought of by Cooley or any of the others gathered in the office.

". . . got to stop 'em," Cooley said. "Raise a posse. Get fifty men. More. It's the only way."

Argument started about the cost of the armored wagon and how it had failed. The banker complained about the cost of a marshal and a half-dozen deputies for a town the size of Thompson and how they only had one deputy left. Slocum almost spoke up to point out that seven men hadn't been successful, even with a fancy Gatling gun and a rolling fortress.

The railroad executive began telling how he was disappointed at the lack of civility and law in Thompson, hinting he might order a different route for the railroad. This provoked a new round of accusations and denials.

Slocum edged out the door, turned, and ran smack dab into a woman dressed in a plain brown gingham dress. She was tall, maybe four inches less than his six feet, and handsome rather than pretty. Her brunette hair was pulled back in a severe bun, and she looked intent. Slocum had seen that look before and it bothered him.

The doctor had rounded up the politicians with a look as steely and severe.

"I heard what Gus said." She took a small step to block

Slocum's attempt to get around her. He bumped up against her chest and felt her full breasts compressing and then pushing him backward as they rebounded.

"Who's that?"

"The deputy. Gus Cooley."

"Never heard his given name," Slocum lied, wanting nothing more than to clear out of town. He wanted nothing more than to be on his way, and getting involved in a conversation would only delay him. "If you'll excuse me, ma'am."

"I'm his wife. Flora Cooley. I found out what you did for him, and he thinks the world of you. You can't forsake him now."

"I've done all I can," Slocum said. "It's up to the doctor to heal him."

"The outlaws. He said there were a dozen of them that left that horrid place in the pass. Where are they? What are they up to?"

"Be glad they're not here," Slocum said.

The explosion knocked Flora into his arms and sent both of them reeling.

10

Flora Cooley stirred in his arms. It took Slocum a few seconds to realize he ought to release her. She pushed up off him. Their eyes met for a moment and she started to speak, then came a second explosion that knocked her flat atop him again. This time Slocum rolled, carrying her with him so that the rain of debris cascaded down on his back.

He saw her lips moving again but heard only distant whispers.

"Deaf!" He knew he shouted but could hardly hear his own voice. Slocum got up and drew his six-shooter. The blasts had come from a few doors down the street. "The bank!"

"I can hear. Stop shouting," Flora Cooley said, sitting up. She didn't bother brushing herself off.

Slocum helped her stand. By now the men in the doctor's office had come out. Behind them came the deputy and a cursing Dr. Radley.

"You can't git up like that, Cooley! I'm not finished with you yet." The doctor grabbed for the deputy, but Cooley was too quick. For a man who had skirted the brink of death, he looked more alive than the others milling about, looking confused.

"The bank," Slocum said, trying to keep his voice down. He wasn't sure he succeeded because the men all jumped and looked frightened—at him, not the commotion going on a couple dozen yards away.

"Must be Silas and his gang," Cooley said. "They bided their time and finally went after the money in the bank."

"I'm being robbed?" This got the banker's attention. Underwood fidgeted with his gold watch chain and shuffled his feet, looking apprehensively down the street where the dust cloud hung in front of the brick building.

"Get a posse together. Roust 'em and be sure they bring guns—loaded," Cooley said. He took a quick look at Slocum, who nodded. Then the deputy went to his wife and gave her a quick hug.

Slocum saw how she recoiled a bit, but that might have been from the way the doctor had bandaged him up. Cooley looked like a walking corpse, but the six-gun he held never swayed.

"You up to it?" Slocum asked.

"I'm all the law there is in Thompson right now. Got to be up for it. You don't have to come along. You know it's Silas and his men."

Slocum cocked his six-gun and started for the bank without waiting to see if Cooley followed. The deputy caught up with him.

"You got more stones than the lot of them," Cooley said.

Slocum lifted his pistol and fired at a masked outlaw coming from the front of the bank. The door had been blown in with the first explosion. The second must have been directed at the vault. All the windows were shattered. From the dust in the air, Slocum guessed the robber was more interested in not breathing that debris than hiding his identity. Robbing a bank at night hardly called for masks otherwise.

The outlaw looked around, startled. Slocum fired again,

winging him. The robber yelped but found the range. He opened fire and forced Slocum and Cooley to dive for cover. Slocum dropped flat on his belly and got off another round that missed but went into the bank. From the inside came a roar of anger.

Cooley stumbled to a doorway and used this dubious shelter to brace his six-shooter for a few quick shots. Slocum couldn't see what the deputy fired at, but none of the shots produced a reaction. Filling the air with lead had advantages, but not too many if he and the lawman ran out of ammunition.

"Get more dynamite. The damned safe's not open yet!"

Slocum recognized Silas's voice immediately. He also saw a box of dynamite in the street. The top of the crate had been ripped open, but he couldn't see how many sticks remained. Silas didn't know a damned thing about blasting. He had used too much to get into the bank and obviously hadn't used enough once he had found the vault.

As the man who had emerged from the bank, only to be driven back inside by Slocum and Cooley, came back out like a prairie dog poking its head out of its burrow, Slocum drew a bead on him. But he didn't fire. Cooley followed his lead, recognizing the need for them to conserve their ammunition.

The outlaw ducked back inside, then burst into the street with his six-shooter blazing. He fired wildly, not coming close to either of the men who ought to have been his targets. All the owlhoot wanted was to retrieve a few sticks of dynamite. Slocum aimed low, waited for the right shot, squeezed the trigger, and hit the outlaw in the thigh as he tried to return to the bank with a half-dozen sticks. The man fell facedown. The dynamite went skittering all over the boardwalk in front of the bank.

Cooley tried to hit one of the sticks, thinking to detonate it. All he did was waste the shots.

"He done shot me, Silas. He hit me!" The outlaw wiggled

like a worm on the ground after a heavy spring shower, trying to get back inside.

Slocum didn't need to kill him. He wanted to shoot another of the outlaws. His chance came fast. A masked bandit looked out to see if he could rescue his partner. Slocum shot him in the face. The only sound was the man collapsing to the floor and then writhing about in the broken glass. Then there was only silence.

Slocum took the opportunity to reload. He still had enough ammo to make the fight interesting if Silas made a break for his horses tethered down the street. The animals pawed and jerked at their bridles, frightened by the blasting and the gunfire. Slocum rolled to the side and pointed to the horses, hoping Cooley would make his way to them and untie them. This would leave Silas and his gang on foot.

The deputy wasn't paying much attention to anything but the bank entrance. Slocum cursed and rolled back to his belly, sighting in on the door, too. He had killed one of the men, but the other he had wounded finally wiggled to safety.

The more he wounded, the better. Silas would have to leave his wounded behind. That might give Slocum a chance to interrogate the prisoners, and he could figure out a way to save Beatrice. Silas wasn't the sort of outlaw not to learn all he could about Galligan, even if he was just riding through.

This got Slocum thinking in a different direction. There wasn't any reason for Galligan to order his men to rob this bank. If anything, that ran counter to what Slocum thought the self-proclaimed emperor's plans were. That meant Silas intended to keep on riding and wanted some spending money for his trouble dealing with Galligan.

"He's making a break from Galligan," Slocum called to Cooley. "He won't be heading back up the pass."

"I figured that, too. You don't shit in your own nest," the deputy said. "Is Silas double-crossing Galligan?"

Slocum fired several times to drive an outlaw back inside.

"They're not going to stay bottled up. Where's the posse?"

"Don't rely on them. The town never supported Menniger, and there's no good reason for 'em to start supportin' me."

Slocum felt suddenly very vulnerable flopped on his belly in the middle of the street. He couldn't wiggle back to safety and standing was out of the question with random shots tearing through the air above him. Lying low, he blended in with the mud and ruts in the street. Give them the chance to outline him against a building or anything bright, like the gaslight pouring from the nearby saloon, and he was a goner.

"No hope?" Slocum called.

"Just us, partner."

"Cover me." Slocum made sure his six-shooter was reloaded, gathered his feet under him, and then launched straight ahead for the bank door.

He got several yards closer before a bullet cut through his side, tearing along his lowest rib and leaving a ribbon of pain and slowly oozing blood behind. Staggering another few steps, he dropped to the ground again and fired straight into the belly of the outlaw who had shot him. The man grunted, then clasped his hands over his stomach, and bent forward as if puking out his guts. When he dropped to his knees, moaning and still clutching his gut, Slocum shot him again. This slug ripped through the crown of the man's hat and probably blew his brains out. When the man crashed to the bank floor, he didn't stir.

"You get another one?"

"Yeah," Slocum called. "How many do you think—" He never got the question out. Two more outlaws blew out from the building, guns spitting foot-long tongues of fire in the darkness. Slocum squeezed off one shot that might have hit

one. Neither man so much as flinched. They were too excited about escaping for a single bullet to stop either of
them. Slocum had heard of men with twenty or more holes
ventilating their hide who still fought and even rode. Not far,
but that didn't matter. Slocum didn't have twenty rounds to
expend.

He pulled the trigger again and his six-gun misfired.

Both men saw him at the same time. Slocum kicked hard
and dived almost parallel to the ground. He crashed into one
man and knocked him into the wall. They went down in a
tangle of arms and kicking legs.

"I got 'im, Jericho," cried the other. Slocum heard the
outlaw's six-gun cock, but then came a flurry of shots that
distracted him.

As Slocum wrestled with the one named Jericho, Cooley
raced across the street to distract the other gunman. He fired
once too many times. His hammer fell with a metallic click
on a spent cartridge.

"No!" Slocum cried, shoving Jericho down as he tried to
shove the other outlaw enough to disturb his aim. From the
solid thunk, the outlaw's bullet had found its target in Deputy Cooley.

Slocum drove his elbow down hard into Jericho's face,
smashing the man's nose to a bloody swamp. Jericho let out
a liquid whine and momentarily lost interest in the fight.
Slocum scooped up the six-gun dropped by the outlaw and
used it on his partner. Then he had to fire repeatedly into
the bank. Silas and another outlaw had come to the aid of
their partners.

Slocum rolled hard, smashed into a post, and managed
to slither around so he came up behind it. The two-inch-
wide support for the roof over the bank entrance wasn't
much to hide behind, but it was all he had. He emptied the
outlaw's pistol in the direction of the door.

Silas left the outlaw who had shot Cooley behind and
dragged in the one Slocum had fought. Jericho cursed

loudly and promised vile things would be done when he caught Slocum. A tiny smile crept to Slocum's lips. Jericho's speech was slurred from having his nose all busted up. Then he realized his own plight. He presented a small target—but one big enough for an expert shot like Silas. Worse, Slocum's six-shooter had misfired. He dragged it out and knocked out the cylinder.

"That's you out there, ain't it, Slocum? You workin' for Galligan?"

"I'm doing this on my own, Silas." Slocum got the punk cartridge out and reloaded. He didn't have time to check to see if the others were properly seated. He snapped the cylinder in and spun it, making sure the mechanism worked.

Or at least he hoped that he had it working again.

"Throw in with me. We got a vault full of railroad money here. Might be a thousand dollars apiece. Why let Galligan get it when we can ride on out with it?"

"He know you're crossing him?"

"Doubt it. He thinks me and the boys rode out to scout where the railroad was surveyin' fer the tracks to come to this town." Silas laughed. "Soon 'nuff, it's gonna be a jerkwater town. They got a coal mine up in the hills to supply fuel and they promised to make the railroad crews real happy, if you know what I mean."

"There's not that many women around town," Slocum said. He cocked his six-shooter and waited for what he knew was going to happen.

"Bringin' in. Galligan's promised all the whores the crews can bed. He's settin' hisself up to be the emperor of not only the pass but everything on either side. That includes this town. He's gonna make himself a real empire."

Slocum fired the instant he saw movement in the doorway. Silas only talked to distract him, maybe to gull him into revealing himself a bit more. The outlaw had no intention at all of welcoming Slocum to his gang since there was no reason.

Silas grunted as Slocum's slug almost hit him. Bits of the doorjamb exploded into splinters and one of them might have caught Silas in the cheek. It was too dark to tell.

Silas disappeared back into the building, muttering to his men.

Slocum knew what was going to come next. They had figured out he was alone. They would rush out and overwhelm him. One or two of them might get hit, but they wouldn't be much worse off then than they were now—and they wouldn't be boxed into the bank.

A quick glance let Slocum locate the box of dynamite. He couldn't run, and he wasn't going to put up much of a fight with only his six-shooter. Standing behind the post, he sucked in a deep lungful of air and then ran as hard as he could before diving to confound the outlaws' aim. He hit the boardwalk and skidded to the opened dynamite. Grabbing a couple sticks, he hunted for fuse and blasting caps but didn't find them.

He stood again, put his foot on the crate, and kicked with all his might. The dynamite skittered to the door and came to a halt just inside. Slocum fired repeatedly into the box until he had only one round left.

"Get it out. Throw the dynamite out!" Silas cried.

Jericho must have been closest. He reached down, picked up four sticks, and for a brief instant presented Slocum with the target he needed. His remaining slug hit one of the sticks in Jericho's hand.

The explosion of the remainder of the case picked Slocum up and hurled him out into the street. He landed hard on his back and kept skidding. The roar and rush of brick fragments passed over his head. He rolled onto his belly and cradled his head with his arms as mortar, flaming wood, and other debris came down on him.

"He blew up my bank. The son of a bitch blew up my bank!"

Slocum shook his head to clear it. His ears rang but the

banker's screams cut through the dying sounds of the explosion in his head. Pushing himself to hands and knees, then to an unsteady stance, feet widespread, he saw the townspeople waving rifles and charging forward.

"Where were you when we could have used you?" he asked. Nobody answered. The banker and the rest surged past him into the bank, now fitfully burning.

Slocum squinted and saw two outlaws dragged out from the bank, still fighting. The explosion had stunned them, leaving them easy prey for the crowd.

"String 'em up. There. That limb's about right!"

Slocum started to complain. He'd put a round through Silas's worthless hide, no matter if the gunman was armed or unarmed, but necktie parties never set well with him. He had been on the receiving end of a lynch mob when he hadn't done anything to deserve it and had barely escaped with only rope burns around his neck. Silas and his henchman deserved to hang, but letting them swing after they'd been tried and sentenced by a judge was the right thing.

No lynching.

"No!" He tried to go after the mob, now pushing and shoving its victims toward the hanging tree.

"He . . . he's dead," came a sob. Slocum turned to see Flora Cooley kneeling beside the deputy. "They killed him."

"He saved my life," Slocum said. He tried to walk, but his legs buckled under him.

Flora spun about, caught him, and together they collapsed into the dirt, Slocum atop her. He tried to get up only to find that the explosion had left him dazed. Strong hands lifted him and then Flora was on one side and Doc Radley on the other.

Slocum felt his toes dragging in the dirt as they pulled him along. More than once he tried to stand but his leg bones had turned to jelly.

"You lie down and rest. Other than that crease on your side, it don't look as if you've been in much of a fight.

Leastways, nuthin' compared to the one you'll be in when Lou finds who blowed up his bank."

"The robbers did," Slocum said, grinning a little. It hurt his face to smile that much so he stopped.

"You stick with that story. Lou Underwood ain't too bright at times, and if he's got his bloodlust all sated by hangin' the varmints in the bank that you didn't blow up, you might be in line for a reward." Slocum winced as the doctor cinched up the bandage on his ribs. "But don't count on it. Lou's so tight he can squeeze a nickel and make the buffalo bellow."

Slocum lay back and the room spun around a mite, then settled down.

"You look after him a spell, Flora. I got my hands full with a couple of broken necks, more 'n likely."

Slocum heard the door slam. He tried to sit up but the brunette forced him back down to the table.

"You heard Doc. You should rest."

Slocum wanted to leave Thompson as quick as his stolen horse would take him. His resolve on freeing Beatrice was fading fast. Even if he got back behind the wall and pretended nothing had happened, Galligan might think he was part of Silas's gang and shoot him out of hand. Or find one of his more inventive tortures for the amusement of the fine citizens of Top of the World.

"Did my husband really save your life?"

"He did." Slocum looked into the woman's eyes, expecting to see tears. Instead he saw . . . something else. For a moment he couldn't figure out what it was and then she kissed him. Hard.

When Flora broke off the kiss, she kept her face close to his.

"I owe you for all you did trying to help Gus. You brought him back alive and the doc was patching him up when . . . when he died."

"I owe him," Slocum said. His head felt as if a wasp's

nest had taken up residence inside. But he wasn't in so much shock that he didn't know what the woman was doing. He felt his gun belt being unfastened and then she worked on the buttons of his fly. "What are you doing?"

"Repaying you for all you've done."

Before Slocum could say a word, her mouth engulfed his manhood. He was half rigid from the way her fingers had fumbled around in his jeans to pull him out. He hardened fast in the warmth of her mouth. Flora's tongue worked in quick circles around the sensitive tip and lifted his hips off the table.

Slocum groaned. This put a strain on his injured rib.

"Sorry," she said. "Is this better?"

She stepped back and wiggled. Her bloomers fell around her ankles. She kicked them free and then stepped up and straddled Slocum's waist.

"You don't do anything. I'll do it all for you."

"To me," Slocum got out as he felt her wet warmth at the very tip of his shaft. Flora rearranged her skirts and squatted down. He sank an inch into her clinging interior. And then he gasped as she relaxed and took him full length.

"Oh, you fill me up inside. You're so big." She pressed her hands down onto his shoulders to hold him in place and began lifting her hips. He felt himself slipping from her, like a spat-out watermelon seed. And then she shoved herself back down and he was once more engulfed in her moist warmth. Muscles tensed and massaged his hidden length until he moaned. This time it was in pleasure. She used tricks he had seldom seen—felt!—before.

Then her hips began to rotate slowly. He stirred about within her and grew even harder. When he reached the point that his erection was so hard he wanted to cry out, she rose and paused. Her face was beaded with sweat and her face flushed. The red flush extended down her neck and across the tops of her snowy breasts.

Just the sight of her heaving bosom and knowing he was

the cause of her arousal almost made him come like a young buck with his first woman.

"You're about the loveliest thing I've ever seen," he said. Slocum groaned as she slowly lowered herself once more. "Or felt."

She laughed in delight and then began rising and falling in a rhythm destined to rob them both of speech. Her every move pushed him a bit closer to losing control. Hot tides rose within him, edged along his length. Steely control held back the flood because he wanted to experience even more. But her determined movement all around him finally took its toll.

His white-hot rush flooded her. Seconds later she cried out, arched her back, and drove her hips down hard into his, as if trying to split herself apart on his fleshy sword.

And then she sank down. Slocum felt himself turning limp and slipping from inside. She rested her cheek against his chest.

"That was mighty nice," she said.

"Was," he agreed. He clumsily put his arms around her, not sure what to do. His head felt like it was going to bust open at any instant and the strength hadn't come back to his legs yet. With the lovemaking she had just lavished on him, he wasn't sure he could do anything but fall asleep, but it was hardly right having her atop him like this.

"Your husband's not dead an hour," Slocum said.

"This is what I needed. A strong man, a man to take my mind off the awful things that happened to Gus. Besides, we never had much of a marriage." She stretched out her legs and completely pinned him down with her weight.

"The doc's going to be back soon," Slocum said.

"You're right," she said reluctantly. Flora sat up, slid her legs together, and dropped off the table. Just then the door opened and Dr. Radley came in, mumbling to himself.

"They got their nerve. They wanted to leave them varmints danglin' fer the buzzards. Had to convince them to plant them out in the potter's field. Used their own saddle blankets. I swear, I think Lou is gonna sell their horses."

"That's his due, isn't it?" Flora asked. She moved cautiously. Slocum saw that she pushed her bloomers on the floor around to get them out of the doctor's sight.

"Ought to be yours," Radley said. "Lou's vault held. Not sure how he'll get the damn thing open since the explosions ruined the safe's lock, but all the railroad money's still there. He lost a building but nothing in the safe. No, sir, not a thing but a building ruined."

Radley cast a gimlet eye at Flora, then at Slocum.

"Thought I told you to rest up," he said.

"You did," Slocum said.

"I need a drink after everything's happening tonight." Radley went to the door, turned, and said, "And you pick up them frilly underpants of yours, Flora Cooley. I don't want to see 'em on my floor in the morning." Chuckling, the doctor left.

Slocum and Flora looked at each other, then laughed. For Slocum, there was an element of hysteria in it, but it burned away the last of his shock. And then Flora made sure he was in tip-top condition one more time.

11

"Why?" Slocum had to ask. He propped himself up on the table on one elbow and looked at the lovely woman. Flora Cooley smoothed her skirts—the same skirts that had been draped over Slocum's waist so she could get unhindered access to his crotch with hers.

"You're a brave man and—"

"Your husband just died. He's the hero. He saved me."

"Gus and I, well, he was out of town a lot," Flora started. She bit her lower lip and looked contrite. "It surprised me that he would give his life for anyone else."

"Much less a drifter?" Slocum asked.

"Oh, no, John. That's not what I mean. Marshal Menniger is the real power in Thompson, and he's just come here not so long ago. The deputies do as they're told, and Gus was one of them. He never showed too much initiative, preferring to stay in the background and go along with whatever the marshal asked of him."

Slocum hadn't seen Cooley that way at all, but maybe she hadn't seen him under such pressure. Cooley had survived the armored wagon rolling down a hill and through force of will had kept himself alive on the arduous trip back to Thompson. Even as bunged up as he was, he'd joined Slocum to go after Silas's gang. The two of them taking on a dangerous man like Silas didn't jibe with what Flora said.

"He might not have been town marshal but he had his eye on the badge," Slocum said. There hadn't been anything definite that Cooley had said, but the way he talked about the job and the town made Slocum think the man's ambitions didn't stop there. A federal marshal roamed a huge portion of western Wyoming and had a great deal more power and responsibility. Again, Gus Cooley had never mentioned it but Slocum had the feeling in his gut that even this might have been nothing more than a stepping-stone for the deputy's aspirations.

"Oh, no, he would have said something about that. All he ever did was ride the circuit around town and serve process. He got paid five dollars for each eviction notice he served. And he didn't do that so much."

"Did he drink up the money?" Slocum thought he knew the answer when Flora hesitated, then shook her head.

"Didn't think so. I bet he salted it away. He might have been a deputy but he probably left you with a fair amount of cash."

"The bank," she said in a low, choked voice. "He had the money in that bank, and the robbers would have taken it."

"He died so you wouldn't starve." Slocum thought Flora might feel bad about what they had just done after he pointed this out to her, but she smiled wanly, came to him, and kissed him with real passion.

"You're so good to take Gus's part in this, John. You've got a heart of gold. You do."

"Doc Radley knows what was going on between us just before he came in. You think he's the kind to talk in his cups?"

"For all his bluster, Radley doesn't say much, and I'm not sure he drinks. That's not something I would really know,

now is it?" She bent, fetched her bloomers, and stepped into them. The look in her eye was devilish. Flora made a big production of turning away, then bending over and presenting her curvy hindquarters to him as she wiggled into them. For a brief instant, Slocum caught sight of what was under the skirts and then they dropped back to a chaste ankle level. When she turned, she was a little flushed. Flora knew exactly what she'd done and how tempting it had been for him.

Had she attracted Gus Cooley in the same way? Slocum wasn't inclined to think on the matter. He heaved his feet off the table and bent forward slightly when his head tried to go in a direction different from his body. The dizziness passed enough for him to try a tentative step or two. The weakness he'd experienced after getting caught in the explosion was about gone now.

He reached for his gun belt and the six-shooter there when he heard loud sounds coming from outside. Slocum stopped, hand still on the butt of his pistol, when Radley came back into the office, followed by the banker and a handful of others.

"Fresh from stringin' up them bastards," one man said.

Slocum had seen men who got a taste of lynch mob violence. For two cents, this one would string up someone else just for the sight of watching his victim kick out his last dance at the end of the rope. Slocum strapped on his gun and felt better for it with a mob like this, no matter that they were likely the town fathers. These pillars of the community were looking for crossbeams to swing more outlaws from.

"Slocum, you tell 'em what provoked Silas to rob the bank."

"*Try* to rob it," Lou Underwood said. "Thanks for keeping the money where it belongs—all safe and sound."

Before anyone else could pipe up, Flora Cooley asked, "There a reward? You paying something to show how valuable it is not letting robbers steal from you?"

"Why, uh, I—" Underwood looked like a frightened deer, eyes wide and darting around to find an escape route. The notion of paying out reward money scared him almost as much as the idea of a robbery.

"Give my share to Cooley's widow," Slocum said. "Mrs. Cooley deserves something for the way the deputy performed his duty so well."

"Well, uh, yes, his duty. You see, Deputy Cooley was only doing what he was already being paid to do. Keep the town safe," Underwood said.

"Lou, you old skinflint," said Radley. "You're gonna be filthy rich when the railroad comes through. You would have lost their trust if that money had ridden outta town in Silas's saddlebags."

"True, but the deputy—"

"I'm not a deputy. I'm no lawman," Slocum said. "Give her the reward."

Slocum spoke with such steel in his voice that Lou Underwood bobbed his head up and down fast and mumbled that he'd do so. There wasn't likely going to be any reward forthcoming, but Slocum guessed that Flora wasn't the kind to give up either. The clash of personalities would have been fun to watch—if he'd intended to stick around town.

"They'll back an assault on the wall," Radley said unexpectedly. "You know all about Top of the World and Galligan. You can get 'em through to rescue my nephew."

"Nephew?" Slocum blinked. His head was still hurting but the buzzing noise had died down. That didn't mean he thought clearly yet or understood what he did hear.

"Marshal Menniger is his sister's boy," the banker said. "They trace back to the early days when Thompson was settled. Menniger just came back after Comstock lit out."

"Me and Henrietta came here with our folks. Ma and Pa died quick, Henny married Sam Menniger, and had three children. Two moved on, one of them became the marshal up in Montana 'fore comin' on back here to do the same job. Couldn't be prouder of him if he was my own son."

Slocum wondered if any attack on Galligan's empire was possible.

"It might be best if you let the railroad executive negotiate for the route over the pass. They got money, they got railroad police if Galligan tries to steal from them or break a contract."

"My nephew's up there now," Radley said forcefully. "These gents are the power in Thompson. They're willin' to back you up if you lead."

"How many men can you muster?" Slocum remembered how quickly the armored wagon had been dispatched by Galligan's guards. Armor plating a wagon and using a Gatling gun had been good ideas, but a handful of men against a fortified position was a sure way to die. Cooley was gone, though his death was only a bit related to all Galligan had done.

Nevertheless, Menniger and his two deputies were still prisoners. And Beatrice. Slocum remembered how she had sacrificed her own freedom so he could escape. He couldn't help comparing the time he'd spent with her, albeit briefly, and with Flora Cooley.

"Menniger's not likely to be alive," Slocum said. "Galligan thinks up new tortures all the time to please himself and feed the town's bloodlust."

"Three days," Radley said. "I reckon my nephew's got three more days. Galligan's celebration of the anniversary of taking over the pass is a big one. He really puts out a spread and kills the fatted calf then. Has for the past two years. Him celebratin' the deal with Bannock and the railroad, fightin' off the law from here, who knows what else will mean he's got to have a big show for his men."

"You think it'll be Menniger and the others who are the main attractions?" For an instant, Slocum's hope flared that Beatrice might be alive. Then it felt as if the weight of the world crushed him down, buckling his knees. If Galligan had left her alive, it was to be used as part of that celebration. Beatrice was a lusty woman, but Galligan was inclined to give her out as a favor to his men.

All of them.

"He might pick and choose among his own men, but having Silas defect like he did is gonna prick his pride. He'll see it as a betrayal—and it was, by his lights. Galligan will want something special, and using men already in Top of the World as showpieces ain't likely to work well."

"There are hundreds of them," Slocum mused. Galligan could abandon one wall and put all his men on the other to defend the town. If another town the size of Thompson had been built at the base of the pass on the other side, right where Corpse River drained into the foothills, attacking one side would work. Draw all the firepower through Top of the World and across the pass, then attack where the guards weren't. But Thompson didn't have a counterpart on the far side. An attack on this side would be met with overwhelming resistance.

"You need a field piece," Slocum said. "Lots of rifles and maybe another Gatling."

"Don't know where Menniger got that," Underwood said. "I certainly didn't give him the money to buy it."

"That's military hardware," Slocum said. "Is there a cavalry post around here? Let them lead the charge."

"Miles off and I suspect Galligan is buying off the post commander."

"Galligan lets military supplies through the pass without collecting a toll," Flora said.

Galligan's position was unassailable without heavy firepower and Slocum told them so.

They grumbled and finally Underwood said, "You find those weapons and we're with you, Slocum."

The men filtered out, still complaining among themselves. Slocum wasn't sure if they were disappointed that there wasn't going to be a full assault right away or if they weren't likely to have anyone else to hang.

"There might be some military ordnance around," Flora said.

"How's that?" Doc Radley looked hard at her. "I never heard of any such thing, and as Lou said, the cavalry commander's snug in Galligan's vest pocket. He won't stir off his fat ass fer love nor money. None that we could give him anyway."

"Gus mentioned seeing a cave up near the played-out mines. He danced around saying what he found there, but it sounded important. He was going to mention it to the marshal but never got around to it, I suspect."

Slocum watched her, wondering what raced through her mind. She thought of a dozen things, no doubt, but were any of them of her dead husband? He couldn't tell.

"Where's this cave?" Radley asked.

"I'm not exactly sure, but I bet we could find it." She turned to Slocum. "John, me and you could go and hunt for it."

Again he felt a twinge of wanderlust—or was it simply self-preservation? This wasn't his fight. Leading a posse of ill-trained hotheads against Galligan's battlements looked to be the quickest way into a grave alongside Silas and his men. Getting Beatrice free might be better done hiking over the mountain and coming down the far side, perhaps near the lake that fed the river Galligan used to get rid of his bodies, and seeing what he could do alone. He had been a captain during the War and had led men into battle who were untrained and lacking in arms. Something told him this foray would be worse than his most horrific battle when it came to counting casualties.

"I got a horse. You, too?"

"Gus has his stabled at Jackson's Livery," Flora said.

Slocum recalled that the lawmen had been in a mule-pulled wagon, so that meant horses were left behind without owners now.

"They're alive, Slocum," the doctor said. "Believe it. Here." He tapped Slocum's chest just above the heart. Slocum winced at the pain from his injured rib. Radley took no notice of that. "When you give up hope, you're givin' up everything."

"Get your horse," Slocum told Flora. "We can hit the trail and be in the hills by sunrise."

"I don't know, John," Flora said, agitated. "One canyon looks like another, and I've never actually been out here. I'm trying to remember what Gus said, but there are so many lightning-struck stumps and abandoned mines."

In his day, Slocum had tried to follow such directions himself, usually without success. He lifted his leg and curled it around his saddle horn, staring down into a long canyon filled with tailings from played-out mines. From what he could tell, silver mining had run its course after no more than a year. A quick examination of the ground revealed nothing important. Twin ruts showed where heavy wagons, laden with ore leaving the canyon and going into the canyon with supplies, had traveled on a regular basis. Weeds overgrew all but the most pronounced parts of the road.

"Nobody's been here in a spell," he said.

"I don't know why Gus would come here either," she said, dejected. "It sounded so good. I wish I remembered more of what he said."

Slocum checked the angle of the sun, got his bearings, and looked at the towering mountain between him and Galligan's empire. Straight through he'd find the waterfall-fed lake with the river bearing the corpses down the far side of the pass. Somewhere over his right shoulder and a half-dozen miles straight through solid rock would be Top of the World.

"There!" Flora stood in the stirrups and pointed. "That rock outcropping looks like an old hag."

"So?"

"Gus mentioned that."

Slocum tried not to laugh. Any hunk of rock could be turned into an old woman or a cow or just about anything a lonely cowboy's imagination could conjure.

"There's a tree growing up into the nose. Gus thought that was about the funniest thing ever. And above it is the cave."

"Caves are all over. If somebody hid rifles in the cave, they had to get there . . ." His voice trailed off when he spotted a road wide enough for a large wagon that led up along the face of the mountain. Without a word to Flora, he swung his leg back over and trotted in the direction of the path. He came to a halt and looked up. The grade was steep but not so steep that a laden wagon couldn't be pulled up by a determined team. He snapped the reins and got his horse moving up the road at an easy gait. Going slowly allowed him to study the tracks, the roadbed, and the mountain itself.

The road climbed higher until it ended just above the stone hag. Looking over the edge of the road showed where the post oak tree had grown upward, seemingly into the stone woman's nostril.

More interesting was the mine shaft leading straight into the bowels of the mountain.

"Doesn't look as if any mining's been done here in quite a spell," he said.

"Maybe they took it all out?" Flora suggested.

"No tailings. There aren't iron rails in the mine to run ore carts. And the mine supports are flimsy." He dismounted and examined the wood holding up the roof. Whoever cut this shaft had used green wood. It sagged ominously as far into the mine as he could see.

"It must go a hundred yards," Flora said. Her voice shook

a bit with emotion. "I . . . I don't like dark places."

"Here," Slocum said, handing her a miner's candle he found on a high ledge just inside the mouth of the mine. He took down another, used a lucifer from his stash, and got two guttering flames to cast pale light.

He didn't wait for her. He advanced slowly, checking the floor to be sure there weren't any pits coming up suddenly. Miners were a crazy bunch and followed ore veins wherever they led. If it was straight down through the floor, they would dig until their fingers bled. Falling into such a pit could be deadly.

But the dust on the floor showed no sign of anyone coming inside in months. He thought he saw faint boot prints maybe made by Cooley some time ago, but animals—probably coyotes from the size of the paws—had obliterated most evidence with their own comings and goings. Holding the candle about waist level, he made his way deeper into the mine.

"Careful, John, you'll bump your head."

He had already discovered the low roof over his head. Rather than keep it at a constant height, the miners had let it drop inch by inch until Slocum was walking stoop shouldered and would eventually have to duck walk.

He stopped suddenly.

"What is it? A bear?"

"Look to either side of the tunnel," he said. "Be careful where you put your candle."

"Blasting powder," Flora said in a low voice. "There're kegs of it."

"Not blasting powder. Gunpowder. For that. For *those*."

He pointed out two mountain howitzers slid into crannies carved from the rock wall. He examined several more of the nooks and found shot, the swab, and everything else necessary to fire the small cannons. The wheels off the carriages were stacked in other alcoves. The 150-pound cannons could be moved from the mine shaft and the limber assembled outside.

"This can throw a twelve-pound ball almost nine hundred yards," Slocum said. "We get closer than that to Galligan's gate and it'll be blown to pieces with a direct hit."

"These boxes," Flora said, excited now. "Ten of them. Each has eight rounds in it."

"Careful. That's gunpowder packed in there with them."

"Two of them. How'd they end up here?" she asked in a small voice.

"They're brass so they're not from the Tredegar Iron Works."

"Is that important?" she asked.

"Iron barrels don't hold up like brass ones." More than once Slocum had seen one of the cast iron barrels rupture during firing, killing the gun crew and sending shrapnel deadlier than anything the Federals delivered through the CSA ranks. "A cannon's good for a thousand firings, or so goes the warning."

He examined the smooth bore but could not tell how heavily used either of the howitzers had been.

"John, listen. Do you hear something?" Flora clutched his arm, breaking his concentration. He started to scold her for letting her imagination run wild, but then he heard it, too. Candle held high, he explored deeper into the mine. The shaft took a sharp turn to the right. In his mind he mapped this out as heading toward Galligan's territory on the far side of the mountain.

"The walls are wet," Flora said, crowding close behind.

Slocum placed his hand on the rock face and felt distant vibration. He pulled back. His hand was damp.

"It sounds like a river," she said.

"Let's get out of here." Slocum wanted to return to town and get some of those willing posse members to drag the howitzers out into sunlight, where he could examine them more closely. Whoever had stashed them in this mine had done so for a reason. Where the cannons had come from or what use they were intended to perform was beyond him, but somebody in Thompson might know.

If the howitzers were in good condition, blasting into Galligan's empire would be a piece of cake. A bit of rifle fire first would draw more of the emperor's men to the wall and then the cannons could be used. With luck, they might take out most of his small army and not have to fight their way into Top of the World.

Radley had said Galligan's big celebration would happen in two days. That didn't give much time to assemble the howitzers, drag them into position, and begin what would be a bloody, dangerous battle.

Slocum stepped out into bright sunlight and took a deep breath. The musty air in the mine stifled him. Slocum turned and helped Flora climb over a few large rocks in the mouth of the mineshaft.

"I'm so glad to be out of that terrible place. But we can use the cannons and—"

He clamped his hand over her mouth. Flora struggled but he was too strong. He whispered, "Quiet." Walking as if the ground had turned to eggshells, he went to the point looking past the stone hag to the canyon floor below.

Four men led their horses along the trail, following his and Flora's tracks. Slocum recognized the leader as Gadsden, the man he had stood guard with the first day on Galligan's toll road. He had been taciturn then but now he was shouting at the three with him as if he was accustomed to giving orders rather than taking them.

"What'll we do, John?"

He didn't know. It wouldn't be long before the tracker found the road leading up to his mineshaft. There wasn't anywhere to run, and Slocum wasn't sure he could outgun four of Galligan's henchmen. They were boxed in and waiting to be captured—or killed.

12

"What are we going to do, John? They're on our trail!"

Slocum's mind raced forward, choosing and discarding ways out. Simply waiting for Galligan's men to find their hoofprints and come up the road was a sure way to die since the road was a dead end at the mine. He toyed with the idea of dragging one of the mountain howitzers out and using that when the four men were on the road, but such defense took time—and he knew it would be only minutes before Gadsden found them. He had not been impressed with the man when they stood guard duty at the eastern wall, but the outlaw was so taciturn that Slocum had gotten little to really create anything but a bad opinion of him.

For all Slocum knew, the man could be the best tracker in the Grand Tetons.

They couldn't stay where they were. There was nowhere for them to run or hide. The ledge in front of the mine shaft was too narrow for much more than the roadbed and a spot for horses to stand, waiting for whoever explored the mine. A quick glance up the side of the mountain convinced him it was too steep a climb to ever get away. The sheer rock

face above the mine would leave them sitting ducks even if
they could climb it.

"We've got to get to the base of the road before they
start up. There's no way I can outgun them," Slocum said.

"Give me your rifle. Together . . ." Flora stopped when
she saw his grim expression. Slocum tried to put on a better
face, but there was no way to swallow this medicine with a
spoon of sugar. It was a bitter fight coming at them fast.

"Let's ride," Slocum said. He swung into the saddle and
made sure the leather thong was slipped off his six-gun's
hammer. When he needed the pistol, he would need it in
a hurry. Until then, the best they could do was gallop downhill, always a risky proposition. The slightest misstep, a rock
that turned a hoof, a gopher hole, anything that broke their
downward momentum, would mean their deaths.

Slocum kicked the sides of his horse and bolted ahead,
tearing down the road. It wasn't far but was long enough to
give Gadsden and his cronies the chance to mount and head
for the base of the road.

The four outlaws were already on the trail. Slocum's
headlong rush did nothing to betray their presence that another minute of tracking wouldn't have revealed. By galloping ahead, he and Flora had gained a hundred yards. That
might be enough to keep from getting trapped on the road.

But it wasn't.

Gadsden let out a whoop and opened fire. The three men
with him were slower to respond but soon enough the air
filled with lead all around Slocum's head.

"Ride," he urged Flora. "Get back to town and let them
know what happened. And the cannons. Don't forget them."
He turned and began coolly firing at the approaching outlaws. From horseback, aiming at men riding hard toward
him—the shots were impossible. Slocum emptied his six-
gun and went for the rifle riding at his knee.

When he opened up with the rifle, his attackers thought

better of pressing their advance. Gadsden dived from his horse and found cover behind a large boulder. Slocum turned the other three with his steady fire, forcing them to retreat.

"Ride, get on out of here," he called to Flora. The woman hung back, as if watching the fight.

"Together, John, we go together."

He cursed under his breath. He was running short of ammunition and couldn't hold back this deadly tide much longer. As if to underline his problems, Gadsden blasted a hole the size of his thumb through his hat brim. It was a lucky shot at this range, but it buoyed the courage of the other three. They wheeled about and reloaded, readying for another charge.

"Come on!" Slocum brought his horse to a gallop over the uneven road when a canter would have been breakneck. The horse strained and occasionally slipped as rocks turned under its flying hooves. A quick glance over his shoulder assured him that Flora was keeping up.

For a few minutes. His horse maintained a powerful, smooth stride but hers began to falter.

"I can't keep up this pace," Flora called out. "Go on, get back to town. Tell them what you must."

Slocum cursed some more, brought his horse to a dead halt, and turned its face. His rifle came easily to his shoulder, and he got off one shot that narrowly missed Flora but hit the approaching outlaw. The man threw his arms up in the air and tumbled backward from the saddle. He had brought down one of the outlaws but the other three came on, heedless now of his marksmanship.

Flora raked her heels along her horse's flanks and then there was no more chance of escape. Both of the horse's front legs collapsed. Its head went between its legs and Flora sailed through the air. She landed hard and didn't stir. For all Slocum knew, the fall had killed her. He fired twice more and then the magazine refused to feed any more cartridges.

With both rifle and six-gun empty, he had no choice but to hightail it.

For a moment, Slocum thought the three outlaws would come after him. Gadsden's sharp command brought back his two pursuing henchmen. Keeping his head down and horse flying, Slocum put as much distance between him and the outlaws as he could.

Only when the horse's flanks lathered and its breath came in huge ragged gusts did he slow and finally walk the horse off the road toward a stand of cottonwood trees. A small pool of water bubbled up from the ground. Slocum let his horse drink while he shoved his head underwater and tried to collect his thoughts.

He couldn't let Flora remain Gadsden's prisoner.

Jumpy as a long-tailed cat beside a rocking chair, Slocum started at every noise. A rabbit poking a nose through a low bush caused him to spin, six-shooter out and cocked. As if knowing his pistol was empty, the rabbit looked at him curiously, then backed away to drink from the pool when it was safer. Slocum began working over what had to be done. Rescuing Flora before Gadsden and the others had their way with her was necessary, but he ran low on ammo.

Checking, he had only twelve rounds left for his gun. He rummaged through the saddlebags on the horse he had taken and found nothing more. His rifle would be better used as a club.

He thrust his head underwater again and let the cold drive away the pessimism. When he came up sputtering, he shook like a dog and sent water droplets flying in all directions. He pulled his horse away from the pool, mounted, and rode back toward the last place he had seen the outlaws. Approaching from an angle, he listened hard for their voices, their horses, any sound Flora might make.

All he heard was the soft wind working its way through rocks and vegetation.

Exploring on foot brought him flat on his belly atop a

large rock. He carefully listened, then sniffed the air and finally stood to cautiously look around. In the distance rose a cloud of dust. He tried to figure how Gadsden had cut across country the way he had, but there was no denying that the outlaws were heading back toward the toll road leading through the pass.

Slocum skidded down the rock, mounted, and set off at as fast a pace as the horse could maintain. He trotted, then walked, and occasionally galloped the horse in an effort to overtake Gadsden. The closest he came was several hundred yards. He pulled his hat low over his eyes and shielded them from the setting sun the best he could.

If he rode like the wind, he could interpose himself between the outlaws and the road leading into the mountains. Try as he might, he could not identify all the riders. He knew the red-and-black-checked flannel shirt that Gadsden wore but could not make out any of the others. If one was Flora Cooley, the outlaws were riding close enough to block his direct view.

A quick estimate of his chances made Slocum despair. Then he bent low on his horse and sent it racing toward a point where he was sure he could intercept the other riders.

By the time he reached the point, going down ravines and up steep inclines, his horse wobbled and was close to dying under him. But Slocum thought he had beaten Gadsden to the road and blocked his way.

After waiting a few minutes and not seeing riders approaching, Slocum began to study the road. A cold knot formed in his belly when he saw evidence that Gadsden had beaten him here and was already climbing the road toward Top of the World.

He tried to get his horse to respond, but he had asked too much of it. Leaving it to rest, he began hiking. The road was good enough that he made decent time, but he reached a bend in the road and looked several switchbacks above him. Flora rode with her head down. In spite of himself, he called out to her. The woman's head snapped up as she looked around, then she was crowded away from the brink.

Gadsden peered down at him. The outlaw vanished, and Slocum saw two riders making the bend just above him. A pair of gunmen rode back to kill him. A dozen schemes flashed through his mind but none gave him more of a chance to survive than simply continuing to walk ahead. Pistol out and held in his hand dangling at his side, he waved with his left hand when the riders were on a stretch of road straight ahead of him.

"I got to talk to Gadsden. It's about Galligan."

The two exchanged looks, and when they did, Slocum raised his pistol and got off four quick shots. Of the three aimed at the rider on his left, one hit, knocking him from the saddle. The other shot went wild but both outlaws' horses reared at the gunfire. This gave him a chance to run a few more yards. By the time he was within range for an accurate shot, the still mounted outlaw was firing at him.

A shot from horseback, even at the best of times, was chancy. Slocum had both feet firmly on the ground and was a crack shot. His first round hit the rider in the leg. As the man grunted and bent toward it, his final bullet caught the outlaw in the chest. Slumping, he tried to wheel about and rejoin Gadsden.

Slocum ran for all he was worth, then launched himself in a dive. His fingers clawed at the rider's legs and came away bloody. The outlaw swung around to shoot Slocum but lost his balance and fell heavily.

Avoiding the dancing horse, Slocum reached the fallen man and kicked him hard. This ended the fight. Panting, Slocum took the pistols from both of his victims and grabbed the last rider's horse. Putting his heels to the horse's flanks, he flew up the road. He had two six-shooters now, but Gadsden was far ahead.

As Slocum came within sight of the wall and gate protecting the toll road, he saw Gadsden herd Flora to the other

side. The gate screeched closed. Galligan hadn't repaired the
splintery mess from where Menniger and his Gatling gun
had tried to blast through it. But damaged though it was,
Slocum had no chance to launch a successful assault against
Galligan's first line of defense.

Guards with rifles popped up on the wall and sighted in
on him. He backed away, then turned and rode, fuming at
how close he had come to mixing it up with Gadsden.

It might have been his imagination but he didn't think
so. In the distance, the far distance on the other side of the
gate, he thought he heard Flora calling, "John! John!"

13

Doc Radley scratched himself, then reached across his desk and opened the far drawer. A half-full bottle of whiskey gurgled as he took it out, withdrew the cork, took a pull, then handed it to Slocum.

"Medicine. I'm perscribin' it to cure what ails you."

"Flora Cooley is Galligan's prisoner. Getting her and the marshal and the deputies free will cure what's eating at me most." In spite of what he said, Slocum took the bottle and knocked back a shot of the potent liquor. It burned all the way down his gullet and pooled in his belly, burning almost as bright as his need to take out Emperor Galligan.

"You got a burr under yer saddle fer somebody who's only passin' through."

Slocum said nothing. He considered another swig of the whiskey but passed it back to the doctor.

"Might be yer one of them poor souls who keeps his promise. Now what'd you promise? And who was on the receivin' end of yer sacred word? You haven't been in town long enough for it to be Flora." The doctor snorted. "She's a character, I tell you. A real opportunist."

"She said Gus didn't have any designs on being marshal," Slocum pointed out.

"She wanted Gus to run for mayor. Lou Underwood's got interests that run a lot beyond the town. His own nest is always in serious need o' bein' feathered. The railroad comin' through is his ticket to a mansion up on the hill— and I don't mean around here. He's thinkin' how nice it would be to have a fancy ass house next to the railroad president's on Russian Hill."

"San Francisco?"

"Nowhere else. That's where the real money is, and it draws Lou like a pound o' raw meat would draw a wolf."

"The howitzer in the mineshaft would take out the gate. Marshal Menniger chopped up the wood with the Gatling gun and—"

"You'll have one chance and that's it, Slocum," the doctor said. "I kin stir up enough passion to get a posse together, but you don't breach that gate on the first try, you've lost them."

Slocum nodded. He understood how mobs worked. A posse was only slightly more organized. He had seen the way they strung up Silas and his men for the sheer bloodlust of it. The crowd hadn't been in jeopardy. Those same men would surge through a gate blown down by the howitzer, but if Galligan's men put up any kind of defense—and Slocum bet they would—that posse would evaporate faster than spit on a hot rock.

"Good that you see what yer up against." Radley sighed, started to take a drink, but stuck the cork back in before dropping the bottle into his desk drawer. "Don't you go get ensnared by Flora. You might say she got Gus killed."

"He was a deputy. I talked to him enough to know he was dedicated to his job." Slocum felt a twinge since Cooley had saved his life. How far that obligation ran after the deputy had died was something of a question for him. He didn't owe Flora anything, but her cries as Galligan's men dragged her away to Top of the World still rang in his ears. Death had cleared the slate with Gus Cooley. What he owed Flora was another matter.

Then there was Beatrice. She had sacrificed herself so he could escape.

"You read him pretty good, Slocum. Hope that cotton wool's not bein' pulled over yer eyes when it comes to his missus."

"I have my reasons for getting Galligan."

"That don't have anything to do with Flora?" Dr. Radley eyed him.

"She's only a part of it."

"Good enough. You want the boys by the gate at dawn tomorrow? I kin get 'em riled up enough by then."

"I need help moving one of those howitzers into place. Three men would be enough, if they know anything about wagons, caissons, or even artillery pieces."

Radley pursed his lips, glanced toward the drawer with the bottle, then fixed his gaze on Slocum.

"I know three men who were in the War. Think they used a cannon. You have any problem with them being Yanks?"

Slocum was past fighting the War and said so.

"I'll git 'em over here. Then it's up to you."

Slocum had known that from the start.

"We got to get the cannon up close," one of the howitzer crew said uneasily. He wiped his lips with the back of a grimy hand. "To get into range, we have to position it where the guards can shoot at us."

Slocum estimated distances and the way the toll road curled around. They had to round the bend, set up the howitzer, and fire before the riflemen found the range and snipers picked off the cannon crew one by one.

"I have some experience," Slocum said. "We get the howitzer loaded and ready to fire, move it up the road, and then fire it."

"Real dangerous doin' that," said another, a short, stocky man with a thick chest and the look of a man used to working at a forge. "I seen cannons go off when the wheels hit a rock. A shock, a spark, sometimes it don't matter. Anything'll set off the charge." He frowned as he looked at the howitzer. "This is a real old barrel. Might explode."

"Might," Slocum said. "And it just might hold. The first shell will send them scurrying like rats. You know how to crew. The next round ought to take out the gate."

"Could work that way," the first man allowed. He looked around. "When's the rest of the posse due?"

Slocum had seen a distant dust cloud on the road below, coming up from town. It wouldn't be long. He went over the procedure for firing, reloading, and firing again. The small man with spectacles and a huge bushy mustache would be the crew chief and aim the cannon, aided by the one who had to be a smithy from the smell of coal and iron lingering about him. Slocum thought he actually had experience while the other two only knew artillery procedures from watching others.

He drilled them over and over, and in less than twenty minutes the posse rode up. Lou Underwood looked uneasy leading the men. Slocum doubted he could be counted on when the hot lead began to fly—and it would, no matter how accurate the howitzer.

"We're ready to attack," the banker called out. "You ready to kick this off, Slocum?"

Slocum didn't answer directly. He went to the mule they'd hitched to the carriage and swatted it on the rump. The mule brayed, then began pulling. In less than a minute, they rounded the bend in the road and the wall with its damaged gate came into view. Slocum had hoped the guards would be asleep on duty and let them set up for their first shot before opening up.

He might as well have wished for the gate to be standing wide open.

Bullets spanged all around as he wheeled the carriage around and unfastened the mule. The animal brayed again and trotted off, leaving Slocum and his gun crew in the middle of the road. The range to the gate was about eighty yards. He stepped back and readied the powder and twelve-pound ball for the second shot, the one that he intended to actually blast down the gate. The first would be for range; the second would open the way for the posse to charge.

He glanced back where Underwood sat astride his horse, looking like he had swallowed a mouthful of bile. Slocum waved. Several of the men signaled back. That was good enough. It had to be.

"Fire when you got things lined up," Slocum told his be-spectacled gun captain.

The immediate roar knocked him back a foot. The man had yanked the lanyard even as he received the order. Slocum waved his arm to clear the air of gunsmoke and saw that the first round had smashed into the wall just above the gate. A couple guards had tumbled over the edge and scrambled to get to the gate, screaming to be let back in.

The second shell blasted from the howitzer sooner than Slocum had anticipated—and the accuracy was everything he could have hoped for from an experienced gunnery crew. The shell smashed into the gate above the heads of the men trying to get inside.

They were hurled away like rag dolls. Best of all, the gate had been ripped off its hinges.

"Charge!"

Whoever screamed the order had seen the damage done and knew they had only a minute at the most to reach the wall. Slocum saw Underwood hanging back, looking fright-ened. When he saw Slocum glaring at him, he swallowed hard, then tentatively urged his horse forward. As he passed the howitzer, the banker joined the shouts of the rest of the posse now at the wall and exchanging gunfire with the guards still able to fight.

"Need a third shot?" The gun captain took off his spectacles and wiped the soot off the lenses.

"Load up but wait to see if it'll be needed to cover our retreat."

"You thinkin' on runnin', Slocum?" The man put the spectacles back on and swiped at his mustache, trying to get it back into a semblance of order.

"Never hurts to be prepared." Slocum considered the chaos scattering Galligan's guards now. The posse had forced its way through the gate and were whooping it up on the other side of the wall. With luck, he could get into Top of the World and find Flora—and Beatrice—before Galligan rallied his men and drove the posse back. When that happened, the third shot would cover the rout he expected.

"If you say so."

Slocum swung into the saddle and galloped for the sundered gate. He ducked as one of Galligan's sharpshooters tried to home in on him. He burst through the gate, then twisted around, six-shooter in hand. He fired three times and one slug hit the rifleman. It wasn't a serious wound but caused the man to stumble. By the time he regained his balance, Slocum was long past.

Slocum slowed his pace to remain behind the dozen posse members who had made it this far. He had counted three lying in the dust along the road leading into the town. Slocum couldn't tell as he rode past if they were dead or just wounded. The wounded would find their way back somehow, and the dead didn't concern him. There was nothing he could do for them when two women were held hostage and needing his rescue.

"Take cover!" Slocum shouted, seeing the trap in the road ahead. Galligan was no one's fool. He had positioned a couple snipers in redoubts along the right side of the road. Emptying his pistol of its remaining rounds bought a few precious seconds for Underwood and the rest of his men.

They scrambled into a ditch and fired into the fortified positions.

Slocum reloaded, sizing up the problem. He wasn't getting past if the posse didn't also.

"There's only the two gunmen," he called to Underwood. "Send four of your men against each position."

Some argument ensued but finally four men advanced on one position while only two went after the second defender. This was all Slocum needed. He slid the rifle from its scabbard at his right foot, cocked it, and waited. The instant the man being stalked by the pair from the posse poked up his head, Slocum fired. A hat went flying and the man sank down.

"He's dead," Slocum called. He didn't care if he had made a killing shot or not. He bellowed out the claim to spook the other defender. And it worked. If two men could kill his partner, four would surely do him in. The man threw down his rifle and fled. Slocum took a couple shots, missing with both. The only effect was to send the man running just a bit faster.

That could work against them if he didn't stop until he reached someone who reported directly to Galligan.

"Get back on your horses. Time's a'wasting!" Slocum shouted. He galloped past, head low. Another bend in the road brought him to a low barricade hastily thrown up by more of Galligan's men. Urging his horse onward, he soared through the air and then landed hard on the far side. The trio of men behind the barricade had not expected this. They spun in confusion to stop Slocum. The posse made quick work of them. Slocum was glad none of the Thompson townspeople had qualms about shooting a man in the back.

He slowed and waited for the posse to catch up to give them another warning.

"There might be more of those varmints ahead, but you've got 'em on the run. Always attack. Keep firing."

Slocum fired up the posse enough that they lit out like somebody'd set fire to their tails. He followed, then found a trail circling around the town. From his memory of the pass and everything in it, this led to the lake that fed the river. Before the day was out, Galligan would have plenty more corpses floating down it. There wasn't a snowball's chance in hell that the posse would get very far into town. Galligan had too many men, all armed, all used to killing.

Even as the thought entered his mind, Slocum heard a roar unlike anything he had heard since the most pitched battles of the War. A hundred rifles firing couldn't have caused louder reports. A cloud of gunsmoke rose as if the entire town had been set ablaze. Then came the cries of pain and the panic he had expected from the men commanded by an indecisive banker more inclined to wage his wars with words and money than bullets.

Slocum caught sight of Underwood and several others—perhaps half of the dozen that had penetrated this far into Galligan's empire—galloping back toward the wall. He hoped his gun captain wouldn't fire the instant he saw them burst forth. Getting killed by enemy fire was one thing but being cut down by your own men was disgraceful.

The echoes from the rapidly firing rifles died down. The stiff breeze blowing through the pass carried away the last of the white smoke over Top of the World.

Slocum dismounted, found a tethering spot for his horse, then went into town on foot to find Flora Cooley and free her.

And Beatrice, too. If Galligan hadn't already murdered her.

14

Sunlight hot on his back, Slocum ducked his head and pulled at his hat brim as he mingled with the crowd. The men all cheered and made bawdy comments about the invasion of their little kingdom. Slocum wondered if Underwood and any of the others had escaped. Then he heard a distant rumble like thunder and knew the howitzer had been fired. He cursed himself for not giving orders to spike the cannon if Galligan's men tried to capture it. The last thing he wanted was for the self-styled emperor to have that kind of firepower.

Whatever deal Galligan made with the railroad, the howitzer would only give him the upper hand. Worse, it ensured that nobody else would ever try to launch an assault against his fortified gate. The cavalry commander was paid off and the people of Thompson would be so demoralized after their defeat that it would be impossible to get two of them willing to try to free their marshal again.

He looked around, saw the jailhouse, and took a few steps toward it, then veered away when Galligan came strutting through the crowd. He had four bodyguards parting the way for him. Galligan tossed silver dollars to the crowd, which roared in approval.

"This is your reward," Galligan bellowed. "You defended Top of the World, you share in the spoils."

Considering the plight of the posse, Slocum knew there weren't any spoils. Galligan was making a big show of throwing a few dollars to the men so he would seem to be the victor.

Another distant roar from the cannon was followed by long silence. Slocum pictured the escape through the blown-apart gate. Underwood and the survivors might not have even slowed to warn the gun crew. Slocum had faith in the gun captain, though, to see what was happening and know there wasn't a point in making a stand.

Slocum turned from Galligan and headed toward the hotel, wondering if Flora and Beatrice might be held prisoner there. He stepped into the deserted lobby and looked around. The room clerk sat in a chair, feet hiked up to the counter. His chin dipped lower until it finally rested on his chest. The sound of his snoring was almost as loud as the howitzer firing.

There wasn't time to search dozens of rooms. Slocum considered looking to see if there was a cellar where prisoners might be kept, but the clerk snorted, swatted at a fly, and almost fell from his chair.

In his best command voice, Slocum barked, "Where're the women? The deputy's wife and Beatrice?"

The clerk's feet slid off the counter with a loud thud, and he fought to catch himself before he tumbled to the floor.

"Wha?"

"The women. Galligan wants them now. The *emperor* wants them for the celebration."

"He move 'em?"

"They're not here?"

The clerk rubbed his eyes and tried to focus on Slocum.

"Never have been, not that I know at any rate. Still upstairs, over at the saloon."

Slocum whirled around and left before the clerk could get a better look at him. He had hoped Galligan would draw most of the men in town to his throne so he could brag on how he had run off another determined force of lawmen, but Galligan had vanished. The men had returned to the saloon, ready to do some serious celebrating.

By the time Slocum crowded inside, the drinks were flowing and there was barely room for him to elbow his way to the bar. He was in dire need of a shot or two of whiskey, but he ignored the longing and made his way through the throng of revelers to a door leading into a back room. He started to open it when the barkeep stopped him.

"Can't go back there. You stay here with the rest. I'm pissed off at how you think you can steal my stock when I'm not looking."

The barkeep was dressed in a fancy ruffled shirt of the kind worn by tinhorn gamblers with his front protected by a white apron. He held a bung starter in his hand. When he saw Slocum didn't obey immediately, he swung it in a hissing arc, back, forth, promising to do to Slocum's head what it did to beer kegs.

"Not looking to steal anything. I was told to fetch the women."

"Upstairs. You outta know that." The barkeep smashed the mallet down hard on the bar and caused several glasses to bounce. Two of the men caught their shot glasses as they sailed into the air. Others weren't as lucky and complained about spilled booze.

"Thought Galligan said they were in the cellar."

Slocum knew the instant the words left his mouth that he'd made a mistake. The bartender's lips thinned to a line, and his eyes narrowed.

"Now why would the emperor say a thing like that to you?"

Slocum shrugged.

"Might be he wanted to get you into trouble," the bar-keep went on. "Why'd he want that, I wonder?"

"I'm just trying to do what I'm told," Slocum said. Shooting it out with the bartender was out of the question when the room was jammed with so many of Galligan's loyal followers. "Why don't you show me where they are?" Slocum glanced over his shoulder in the direction of the stairs leading to the second floor. A Cyprian was making her way down but didn't get too far before getting accosted by a pair of men, both halfway drunk in spite of the early hour.

Their condition didn't bother her. She took both of them back up the stairs with her. As she sashayed up, Slocum saw she wasn't wearing anything under her skirt. That made for quicker turnaround with the customers, Slocum reckoned.

"That's Lil," the barkeep said, the mallet still clutched in his ham-sized fist. "She the one you want?"

"Could be," Slocum said. "Why don't you give me a shot of whiskey?"

The barkeep reached down and started to pour from a bottle at hand but Slocum shook his head and said, "Not that. The good stuff. This is supposed to be a celebration, isn't it?"

The instant the bartender turned to find a bottle of better whiskey, Slocum stepped back into the crowd and let himself be carried out of sight. If Flora was in the back room or upstairs, it would take more for him to find her than it was worth. He had to be in condition to rescue her, and the barkeep pretty much guarded the entrance to her prison.

If she was in the back room at all. Slocum had no proof that she was. Worse, he had no idea where Beatrice might be kept. All he had gotten was a vague snippet of information from the desk clerk at the hotel. For all Slocum knew, the man was more asleep than awake when he'd revealed Flora's location. Still, that convinced Slocum he hadn't been sent on a wild-goose chase. The man had been too drowsy to think straight and had blurted out the truth.

The crowd surged, and Slocum floated along on the tide of humanity like a leaf in a running stream. The unpleasant memory of the bodies floating down the river haunted him. He let the men work him toward the doorway so he could get outside and see if there might be a window in the back room he could enter. If nothing else, he might peer through and actually find where Flora Cooley was being held. When he knew that, he could make better plans—ones that might even succeed in the face of so many of Galligan's followers.

Barely had he let himself be carried outside when everyone around him froze. The men started slipping away, following the front wall of the saloon in both directions as if going into the street meant death.

"Grab them sons of bitches. They ain't gettin' outta doin' their share of work 'round here."

Slocum couldn't see who spoke, but from the tension growing in everyone around him, he knew it had to be one bad hombre.

"Them. Those ten." The command was punctuated by men using riding crops to swat and herd everyone around him. Slocum found himself moving as if he had been trapped in the middle of a flock of sheep.

He winced as the leathery old galoot whacked him with a quirt. He spun and faced the man before he realized he was drawing attention to himself. As he tried to dissolve back into the crowd, the man lashed him across the chest with the quirt. The welt it raised on his skin smarted, as if the leather whip had been dipped in acid.

"Don't," Slocum said.

"You all big and tough. You get on over there with the work detail."

"Having problems, Whitey?"

"Not that I can't handle." The old white-haired man reared back to lash Slocum again.

Four men approached, all carrying short whips. Behind them were more of Galligan's gang, all carrying sawed-off shotguns. Whatever trouble Slocum started would quickly end with him dead in the street. If any of the men with scatterguns opened up at this range, more than he would be cut down. Slocum reflected on how this wouldn't matter much if he was turned into ground meat by the shotgun pellets.

"Didn't mean anything," Slocum said, putting down his head. Trying to look contrite was impossible. He backed off, seething.

"Work detail. You get to help rebuilt the west wall and gate. Those stinkin' bastards blew it to hell and gone with a cannon."

Slocum wanted to ask if the howitzer had been captured but refrained. He would find out quickly enough. He turned and let the old man shove him along, now and then using the short whip to keep him moving.

"Hold up," came a voice that sent chills up Slocum's spine. He reached for his six-shooter but sudden pain shot up his forearm when the white-haired man whacked him good on the wrist. "Is this the one?"

"Yes, Emperor, it is," Whitey said.

Slocum knew he had to make a break now. He lowered his shoulder, drove forward hard, and caught the old man in the belly. He collapsed like a house of cards in a whirlwind. Slocum spun around and clumsily grabbed for his six-gun using his left hand, only to find himself grabbed and securely held.

He was spun around to face Galligan.

"Wondered who had the stones to wheel a damned cannon right up to my front door, then use it to blow his way in. How the hell have you been, Slocum?"

"Too bad the range wasn't right. One of those shells ought to have blown you to smithereens."

Galligan chuckled.

"You have quite a sense of humor. Normally, I'd send

you along with the gate repair crew, but I'm not sure I trust you. That attack was mighty effective, yes sir. Putting you that close to freedom might—"

"Might let me get the hell away like Silas and his gang?"

Slocum saw the storm clouds of anger forming around Galligan at the taunt. He had been right that Silas had double-crossed his boss, thinking to steal the railroad money and then hightail it.

"I'll find that son of a bitch," Galligan snarled.

"Too late. He got his neck stretched for trying to rob the bank down in Thompson," Slocum said. His shot in the dark had struck a new target. Galligan turned livid and began to sputter.

"I wanted to shoot him myself. How dare they execute him? I wanted to invite him to a bonfire."

Slocum tensed. If Galligan couldn't send a kerosene-soaked Silas down a line of men with torches, Slocum might be an acceptable substitute.

"You'd have liked to see that, Slocum. Trust me. I know you want me to think you like me. All goody-goody when you're talkin', but when nobody's lookin', you're as big a thief and—" Galligan began sputtering again.

"What you want done with him, Emperor?" Whitey tapped his quirt on Slocum's chest, looking for the welt so he could add to the agony. Slocum put on his best poker face. Any show of pain would only encourage Whitey—and Galligan.

"Shackles. Get him in shackles, then take him out to the lake. There's plenty of work for a *gentleman* like Slocum." Galligan openly sneered at him as a quick hand plucked the six-shooter from his holster and others gripped him too tightly to fight. He was shaken from side to side as they steered him away from their boss.

"Davidson, get another pair of shackles on these ankles," Whitey said.

The blacksmith lumbered out of his forge, wiping his

hands on a dirty rag. He gave Slocum the once-over, then silently pointed to a bench. Slocum's captors roughly shoved him down onto it, and within fifteen minutes he had iron cuffs locked around his ankles, held together by an eighteen-inch length of chain.

"Don't know why Galligan is bein' so easy on you," Whitey said. "Most men who cross him the way you did get their comeuppance real quick."

"He's the one that got out of the rat pit," another of the outlaws said. "I seen him use a rattlesnake like it was a whip. He—"

"I heard," Whitey said. Slocum saw the old man walked with a slight limp. Under ordinary circumstances, he could run faster than the arthritis-wracked old geezer, but with his ankles chained together, he didn't have a chance.

He was loaded into a wagon bed, two men watching him like hawks. Even if he overpowered one of them, the other would gun him down. Whitey drove and made no effort to avoid the rocks in the roadbed. Slocum found himself being tossed around and finally gave up even trying to brace himself. He rolled about and bided his time. The guards would flag or Whitey would hit a chuckhole and give him his chance.

Only that chance never presented itself. The wagon rattled to a halt not twenty yards from the lake.

"You get the plum job," Whitey said. "Get to it."

"What am I supposed to do?" Slocum turned to see another wagon heaped with bodies. It came to a halt close to the lakeshore.

"Figure it out, smart guy. Throw the bodies into the lake. Make sure the current catches them so the river washes them down east of here."

Slocum was shoved and prodded to the other wagon. He grunted as he hefted a dead body over his shoulder and carried it like a sack of flour to the lake. Grunting, he heaved it into the water, where the strong current swept the corpse away. Within a minute, it had vanished from sight. By then Slocum was struggling with a second body.

He worked until past sundown emptying the wagon of its grisly cargo. Then he wondered what was in store for him. Whitey and two others spread out as they approached him. Slocum waited to fight for his life and vowed that at least one of them would have his body added to the stream of carcasses tumbling down the river.

But with the shackles hobbling him, he knew there wasn't much hope of that.

15

"Wake up. You're not gettin' no day off when there's still work to be done."

A hard toe poked Slocum in the ribs. He winced. The wound was healing but still tender. He looked up at the guard, who stood above him grinning ear to ear. It took him a few seconds to remember how they had beaten him unconscious the night before.

"We got some folks to help you today, Slocum. And it's a good thing." He jerked his thumb over his shoulder.

Slocum lifted himself up off the cold ground where he had slept without a blanket. There wasn't a bone or muscle that didn't ache, but the sight of another wagon rattling up made him forget his misery. In the back of the wagon were a dozen more corpses. And riding with the dead were three people. Two men and Flora Cooley climbed down. The woman staggered away from the wagon, then fell to her knees. Slocum saw she had been shackled just as he had been.

"They're going to help out? You have that many bodies to get rid of?"

"Reckon so. That was one fierce fight we put up." The guard looked uneasy and motioned for Slocum to stand. Something had happened that made the man just a tad frightened. Slocum wanted to find out what it was. If one was scared, more in town would be also. He could play on that fear to rescue Flora and Beatrice.

He snorted in disgust as he got to his feet. Finding Flora hadn't gone too well for him, and now she was one of the chain gang ordered to carry the bodies to the lake.

"You and you," the guard ordered, pointing to Slocum and a man so thin he disappeared when he stood sideways. "Start movin' them bodies to the lake."

"I . . . I'm not feeling too good," the other prisoner said. "Can't hardly focus my eyes." He turned his head, and Slocum saw what might be the reason. A bullet had entered the man's skull and didn't seem to have come out anywhere. If it had, it would have killed him outright. Leaving the bullet in his head only slowed the death sentence.

"I can—" That was as far as Slocum got before the guard slammed a rifle stock into his back. He stumbled forward and fought to stay on his feet. Clumsily turning, fists clenched, he would have swung at the guard except for the rifle leveled at his midsection.

"Got orders not to take any guff off any of you convicts," the man said, grinning. An upper front tooth had been knocked out. The other had been replaced with a gold tooth, giving him a comical appearance. There was nothing funny about the way his finger curled on the trigger.

Slocum saw the knuckle turn white with tension. Only a small added pull would send a slug driving into his gut.

"We got work to do," Slocum said to his wounded partner. The two of them hefted a body. From the look of it, shrapnel had sliced through the man's throat, and he had bled to death. As they neared the lake, his partner began to flag and finally sank to his knees. Slocum followed him down.

"Can't go on. My head is hurting so bad."

"What happened?" Slocum pointed to the corpse's throat.

"Rushed after the posse from the town. Into mouth of cannon. Three, four rounds. Killed a lot. I . . . I tried to get out and got shot." His hand reached for his temple. He turned white and slumped over the body he had just helped Slocum carry.

There wasn't much need to check, but Slocum did anyway. The man was dead from his head wound. Why he hadn't died outright was something Slocum considered a small miracle, but he had seen it during the War. Men with arms and legs blown off and still fighting. Only after the battle did they realize what had happened. Most had died. Some hadn't.

"He kicked the bucket, huh? Toss him in after the other one." The guard held his rifle in the crook of his arm but could swing the muzzle around easily and add Slocum's body to the pile. The guard spat into the lake. "Lookee there. Water's turned downright red from all the bodies. Last time I saw it like this was right after the emperor took over."

"Took over?"

"Was some owlhoot here first. He didn't want to charge passage through the pass. Big fight." The guard spat again. "I picked the winner and here I am now three years later. And there you are." He motioned with the rifle for Slocum to get to work.

Rolling first one body and then another into the lake proved more difficult than Slocum had anticipated. The muddy shoreline had turned to muck from so much blood being added to the dirt. He finally got one body floating toward the outflow but the shackles on his dead partner carried him down into shallow water.

"You get him on out into deeper water."

Slocum waded into the lake, shivered at the cold water, and almost lost his balance as a powerful current caught at his legs and waist. He heaved and got the shackled body into a pool that swallowed it up quickly. Whatever fish there were in the lake would dine well on human flesh.

"Don't dawdle. You got more work to do."

Slocum slogged his way back to the wagon, where Flora struggled with a body weighing half again what she did.

"The two of you, you're a team." The guard laughed. "Honey child, he's not gonna be your first." The guard laughed even harder until tears came to his eyes.

Slocum put his finger to his lips to silence Flora. The less Galligan's men knew, the better. It didn't seem that the guard realized they knew each other—or that Slocum had launched the attack to rescue her.

"She's out here to do some work 'fore the emperor gives her to his men. All of them. You gettin' ready for 'em, honey child?"

"Gadsden turned me over to Galligan to get in good with him," Flora said bitterly. "He took it into his head to make me an example for everyone down in Thompson."

"She's the wife of Menniger's deputy. The marshal's got a big mouth. Otherwise, we'd never have knowed that."

Slocum judged the distance to the gloating guard and realized every word out of the man's mouth was intended to provoke. He wanted to shoot Slocum down, maybe with a bullet to the leg to slow him. Everything about Galligan and his men had to do with torture.

"They're trying to spook you," Slocum said softly.

"It's working," Flora whispered back.

"Hey, there, none of that. You two get to work."

After following them back and forth to the lake a couple times, the guard found himself a spot under a tree where he could watch them work. Neither could escape with the shackles fastened on their ankles. If he'd had time, Slocum might have picked the crude lock on the leg irons, but he'd need a knife or ice pick to begin. And he couldn't have the guard watching. It might be better to find a rock and just smash the lock.

"I have a key," Flora said softly as they carried another body to the lake.

"Where'd you get it?"

"Took it off a body. A guard. He must have worked in the jail but got himself killed by somebody from Thompson." She smiled weakly. "You came for me, John. I didn't think you would."

"The howitzer worked just fine, but we needed more men."

"I heard Galligan ordered a counterattack and the cannon chopped 'em up something fierce."

"Hey, you two, quit lollygagging. Get to work!"

"If I distract him, can you get your shackles open?" Slocum asked.

"It'd be better if you—"

The guard swung his rifle and caught Slocum on the side of the head, knocking him to the ground. "I said no more talking." He turned to Flora and leered. "I want you first. I want to hear you cryin' out for more of what I can offer. The rest can do whatever they please with you."

"Yeah, you want me? Take me now," she said.

Slocum blinked hard, trying to get his senses back. Flora held out bloody hands, stained from carrying corpses. She beckoned to the guard. Slocum fought to keep the buzzing out of his head so he could take advantage of the trap Flora was setting for the guard. The instant the man went to rape her, he had to have his complete attention on her.

Slocum could jump him then.

Try as he might, his legs wouldn't move. He moaned to get Flora's attention, but the guard blocked his view—and Flora's view of him.

The sound of horses approaching caused the guard to stop.

"Damn," he mumbled. "That old son of a bitch has a way of messin' up my fun."

Slocum twitched and twisted around to see Whitey and

three others on horseback. The old man shouted and the guards left their charges to gather around.

"John, the key! I dropped it." Flora dropped to hands and knees and rooted around trying to find the precious key.

Slocum groaned and forced himself to join the hunt. This lasted only a few seconds. Strong hands lifted him and spun him around. Whitey had ridden over and glared at him.

"You look like a dog sniffin' 'round, Slocum." Whitey looked at Flora, who had given up her hunt for the key and sat on the ground, glaring up at her captor. "That's a good piece of ass to be sniffin' after but it ain't yours. Get her cleaned up in case the emperor wants her 'fore he gives her to the rest of us."

"When are you going to do that?" Flora cried. "Or are you just blowing smoke?"

"It'll happen. Wait and see. Think on it." Whitey jerked at the reins and galloped off, the men who had come with him following behind. As they rode past, each gave Flora a lustful look.

"They're trying to frighten me," Flora said. She sniffed. "They're doing a good job."

She yelped when their guard dragged her to her feet. As she stood, both she and Slocum saw the key. It had been caught in the folds of her skirt and now fell to the ground on a patch of grass. Slocum was too far to grab it, but it was at Flora's feet. Gathering his strength, Slocum launched himself. He was weak and his legs refused to work right but he hit the ground and rolled into the guard's legs.

Slocum winced as a spur cut into his arm. His attack had been so pathetic that the guard wasn't even unbalanced, but he did turn to take a kick at Slocum. The toe of the boot landed in his belly and all the fight went out of him. By the time Slocum regained his breath, the guard was dragging Flora off. Slocum hunted for the key but couldn't see it. He wasn't sure if she had retrieved it.

"On your feet. You're not gettin' out of work that easy."

A strong hand on his collar lifted him. Another guard replaced the one who had dedicated himself to Flora.

The guard took him to the far side of the lake and shoved him down.

"We need some rock to build in town. You and the rest will pile up the stones, then load it all into a wagon when it's brought around."

Slocum looked left and right. Three others were there.

"Howdy, Marshal," he said. "I thought you'd be dead by now."

"Both deputies are," Menniger said. His face was covered with bloody scratches and dirt. His right arm was in a crude sling made from his coat. Mockingly, his badge had been used to pin the sling to his shirt.

"I got Underwood to lead an attack."

"Heard a howitzer firing. That must have been quite a sight. I saw how scared it made Galligan and the others. He thought the cavalry commander had turned against him." Menniger snorted. "There's no chance that pusillanimous son of a bitch would ever get unbought."

"Might if the price was right—if Bannock offered him enough."

"Bannock is willing to pay off Galligan. He thinks Galligan's an honest crook and will stay bought."

Slocum dropped to his knees at water's edge and began cleaning off the gore on his shirt and pants.

"Your attack must have killed a couple dozen of 'em," Menniger said. "Wish I coulda seen it."

"Wish you could have been there shooting at Galligan's men with the rest of us."

Menniger thought for a moment, then said, "Joining in a fight doesn't sound like Underwood. He gettin' that desperate?"

Slocum explained how Silas had tried to rob the bank and the way that had ended.

"So Cooley's dead. Shame. He was a good man."

"You ever hear him talk about being mayor?"

"Gus?" Menniger laughed at such a notion. "He didn't even want my job. Why'd you ask?"

Slocum explained what Doc Radley had said about Flora.

"She's something of a mystery to me. Great-lookin' filly but what she saw in Gus is beyond me."

"He was a brave man. Saved my life by giving up his own."

"Now *that* sounds like the Gus Cooley I know. Knew. He believed in duty and doin' his job as good as he could."

They started working to pull up the rocks from the muddy ground and pile them, knowing the guards would shoot them where they stood if there weren't collecting stones for whatever project Galligan had in mind. Slocum's entire body ached but somehow work took his mind off it after a while.

Once he stared at the lake. The blood from the bodies had been washed clear, giving the lake a peaceful, crystal-clear look.

"Is that waterfall coming from the side of the mountain what feeds the lake?" He looked around. The lake sat in the middle of this valley without obvious feeders other than the waterfall.

"Underground river, more 'n likely comin' out of the hills," Menniger said. "Never gave it much thought."

Slocum moved more rocks and considered the rushing water he had heard in the mine shaft where Flora had shown him the howitzers. That water had to go somewhere, so why not through the mountains and somehow come out the side of the mountain, feeding the lake and giving rise to the swiftly flowing river?

"We got company," Menniger said. He ran his arm across his forehead. The shirt rolled up on his forearm came away bloody from all the cuts that refused to close because of the sweat and dirt.

Slocum watched the wagon rumble up. His heart skipped

a beat when he saw Flora riding in the bed. She pointedly ignored him because of the two guards riding with her.

"Get the wagon loaded." The guard closest to Flora shoved her out of the wagon. "You, too. You been malingering all afternoon."

From the woman's disheveled look, Slocum doubted that. What they had her doing was another matter. It hadn't been piling up rocks, though Slocum guessed she would have preferred that. Without so much as exchanging greetings, they toiled side by side to get the rocks loaded into the wagon.

"You're lucky I got a heart of gold," the guard said. "I'm lettin' the lot of you ride back."

There was hardly room but Slocum and Menniger crowded in. The guard had Flora join him and the driver. The other guard braced himself against the side, feet pressing into the rocks so he could keep his balance. Slocum expected the driver to keep going with them all the way into town. To his surprise, the wagon creaked to a halt near the lake where they had thrown in the bodies that morning.

"You out." The guard slapped the driver on the shoulder and said, "Come on back with the next shift 'fore midnight, will you?"

Slocum couldn't hear what the driver said but the guard glared at him, then jumped down. The wagon rattled off toward Top of the World.

"Thought they'd have us unload the stone," Menniger said. "Just as well. Can't hardly lift my arms."

"You need those cuts cleaned. The water in the lake ought to be clean by now."

"Yeah, go wash off that ugly face of yours," the guard who had ridden with them in the wagon bed said.

"Go with him. Don't want no trouble." The guard Slocum pegged as the leader—the one Whitey spoke to rather than the others—pointed.

"Ah, hell, what's he gonna do? Run away?"

Menniger and the guard went to the lake, leaving Slocum, Flora, and two others. The men with them curled up and were asleep in seconds.

"We getting fed?" Slocum called.

"You ain't done enough work to earn your feed," the guard said. "Not even she has." He leered at Flora.

Slocum was taken by surprise when the woman rolled over several times until she pressed hard against him. She reached up and kissed him hard on the mouth.

"Stop that. You save that for the emperor! Hell, save it for me!"

The guard grabbed Flora and dragged her away. Slocum watched but didn't call out. When she had kissed him, her tongue had parted his lips—pushing the key to his shackles into his mouth.

16

"You come on along now, honey child," the guard said, dragging Flora away.

Slocum lounged back, trying not to react prematurely. Only when the guard had disappeared with Flora did he push the rough-edged iron key from his mouth and spit it into his hand. He held it for a moment, warm and hard and full of the promise of revenge. He brought his knees up and reached down to fit the key into the lock. For a heart-stopping moment he thought Flora had given him the wrong key. He strained and worried that the key was bending from the pressure he placed on it.

The click was so loud he recoiled as if it had been a gunshot.

Slocum kicked and got the shackle off his ankle. He used the key to open the other lock. For the first time since he had been caught, he was free. Free to do what had to be done.

He rolled over and got his knees under him. He stood slowly, not wanting to draw attention to himself. From the sounds coming from behind a nearby bush, he knew what was going on and why the guard had taken Flora away.

Walking gingerly, afraid he might step on a rock or dried twig and give himself away, he made his way to where the bush shook. When he reached them, he knew he could have come up beating a drum and the guard would never have noticed.

Flora was on hands and knees, her skirt hiked up and the guard taking her from behind like an animal. The guard made odd noises, but Flora only groaned. Slocum positioned himself, circled the guard's neck with his brawny forearm, and then jerked back and up as he tightened his grip. The guard didn't know what was going on for an instant. This was all it took Slocum to finish him off. He turned and heaved, discarding the man like the offal that he was.

"John?" Flora's voice cracked with strain.

"Let me get you free." He dropped to his knees and worked the key in the woman's shackles. These locks opened more easily than his, as if they had been oiled more often. "There."

"I didn't think you'd come so soon."

Slocum scooped up the guard's six-shooter and rifle and pulled the quirt from his belt. He wished he had his own six-gun but these weapons would do for what he had in mind.

"He's dead?" Flora looked at the dark, still guard stretched out on the ground.

Slocum swung the quirt as hard as he could across the guard's face. No twitch, no movement, nothing.

"Dead," he pronounced.

"What are we going to do?"

"Been thinking about that. We free the others and try to bull our way through town. That's the only way to get to the gate leading to Thompson."

"The eastern gate might not be as heavily guarded," Flora said.

"True, but it's weeks around through another pass to get to Thompson."

"I don't have to go back. I'll go anywhere with you."

Slocum barely heard her. Galligan had done things that could never be forgiven. The only way of stopping the arrogant self-styled emperor was to rally the men in Thompson once more. From the number of bodies he had thrown into the lake, Slocum knew Galligan couldn't have as strong a support in Top of the World as he once had. The howitzer had robbed the outlaws of their feeling of invincibility.

The second one would send them running like cockroaches.

"The marshal is over by the lake. The guard dragged him off to get cleaned up. With him, we can free whoever else has survived out here."

"John, we don't have to fight Galligan. There's no shame in running."

He looked at her as if she had grown a second head.

"We free Menniger and then see what needs to be done."

He shrugged off her grip as she took his arm. The idea of justice wasn't too well instilled in all people. Stride long, feeling good that he didn't have to shuffle along with the chains on his feet, Slocum reached the dark shoreline quickly. The moon had yet to rise and the starlight was muted by high clouds racing across the sky.

The soft sound of water lapping against the shore drowned out most other noises. He looked first one way and then the other to find Menniger and the guard with him. Small, indistinct shapes moved at the edges of his vision. Coyotes or wolves. But Menniger and the guard were nowhere to be seen.

He spun, rifle lifting, when feet hammered against the ground. Flora waved her arms wildly but did not call out as she approached. She flung herself against him and held him tight.

"Guards. Lots of them coming from town."

"Whitey with them?"

"The old man with the white hair? Yes, he was leading them. At least five others coming out from town. It won't be long before they find the guard you killed."

Slocum looked around once more hoping to spot Menniger. He needed the marshal now more than ever.

"We have to make a run for it," he said, coming to a conclusion. Menniger was on his own.

"Where? Whitey is between us and town."

Slocum had worked all afternoon at the far side of the lake and had studied the tall, sheer rock walls. This small lake almost filled the entire pass, save for the space along the road occupied by Top of the World. He grabbed Flora's arm and pulled her around the lake edge.

"We have some climbing ahead of us," he said. "On the other side of that peak is the mine where we found the howitzer. We get over the mountain, and it's not that far into town."

"That's a tall peak," Flora said in a tiny voice.

Slocum heard the sounds that warned him Whitey had found the opened shackles. It wouldn't be long before he organized his men and started a hunt. Unless Whitey had a reason to go back.

"You head straight for that hill. You see the one?" Slocum pointed and then shoved her on her way.

"What are you going to do, John?"

He heard the question but didn't answer. He gripped the rifle and went to find a spot where he could put a touch of fear into Whitey's soul. Almost back to where he had gotten free, Slocum saw two men outlined by a campfire. Whitey had built it to better muster his men. He couldn't know it was also going to help one of the best marksmen the CSA had trained.

Slocum lifted his rifle, aimed, and squeezed off a shot. The report echoed through the narrow valley, hiding where the shot had come from. One man half turned and then collapsed to the ground. The outlaw with him stood, stunned. He joined his partner a second later.

Slocum wanted to go after the rest, but Flora had said Whitey had led a half-dozen men. Two down, four to go. But now they knew he was in the dark, gunning for them.

As much as he hated to quit the battlefield, he melted back into the darkness. When he reached the lake, he broke into a run using the hill he had pointed out to Flora as his guidepost. In less than fifteen minutes he overtook her. Flora was panting and had obviously run herself to the point of exhaustion.

"John, it's you! I heard shots."

"There's two less of the bastards," he said. "We have to keep moving. Whitey will be after us as quick as he can."

He half supported her until she got her wind back, then they walked along at a clip just shy of a run. From the stars, he read that it was well after midnight when they reached the hill. Behind the dark mound of rock was the vertical face of stone leading to the top of mountain.

"We can't climb that," she said. "They'll see us for sure."

"I haven't heard sounds of pursuit. It might be that Whitey figures he can track us better in daylight. That means we've got a few more hours before he comes for us."

"I can't go on," she said.

"There. See it?" He traced along a dark line halfway up the rock face. "That's a ledge. We get to it and we can rest."

"It's so far," she said. Then she unexpectedly turned and kissed him full on the lips. The brunette melted into his arms, and he felt himself responding in spite of their predicament. Her tongue danced along his lips and teased his tongue. And then it was gone and so was Flora.

She dashed to the trail leading upward and beckoned to him.

"Race you up."

Slocum shook his head. Whatever it took for Flora to

find the strength to continue, he was all for it. He trailed her up to the narrow, rocky ledge, occasionally looking out over the lake. All he saw was the deeper darkness of the shoreline, starlight reflecting from the surface of the water. No movement, no sign of pursuit. Whitey might let them go, thinking the escape of a pair of Galligan's slaves meant nothing, but once he reported to the emperor, that would change. Slocum had seen men like Galligan before. He was not capable of admitting defeat, and losing any of his prisoners meant a personal failure.

Whitey and a lot of others would be on their trail eventually. Slocum hoped to make it to the top of the mountain and down the other side to Thompson before that happened. He found it difficult to lift one foot and put it in front of the other. His backbreaking, soul-chilling work coupled with not having been fed wore on him as much as the steep path.

He was drifting a bit when he came to the ledge where Flora had stopped. She had already dropped down to rest, and he wasn't paying close enough attention. Taking a tumble forward, only his quick reflexes saved him from falling full on top of her.

She put her arms up and circled his neck, pulling his face down to hers.

"You've got the right idea, John." She kissed him.

He sagged a little and pressed against her firm breasts. Tired as he was, he found this exciting him and sending blood racing through his veins. He relaxed and let his weight crush her even more. She did not protest. If anything, this caused her to become even more aggressive, kissing and running her fingers through his hair after she knocked off his hat.

"I want you," she whispered hotly.

"You're a marvel," he said. "After everything you've been through the last couple days, you—"

"I want this!"

Her fingers ran down across his belly and wormed under his jeans. The tips of her fingers touched his manhood.

He had been responding. Now he snapped entirely erect—painfully erect—trapped in his tight jeans. He moaned and excited her even more.

"Let me get you out where you can do us both some good," she said.

Slocum felt the buttons on his fly pop open one by one. For only a brief instant when he was free did the cool night air surround his hardness. Flora's hot hand circled him and began working up and down. He kissed her while she continued moving on him, getting him to a steely length that throbbed with need for her.

He rocked back a little, his knees between hers so he could slide his hands down to his waist, to her hips, under her skirt, and across vibrant, creamy smooth flesh. He felt her ass lift off the rock as she wiggled around to get her skirt bunched up at her waist and out of the way. His hands slipped between her thighs, gently pushing them apart.

"Oh," she said as he spread her wide open. Flora lifted her knees on either side of him, then she cried out as he positioned himself and pressed the plum tip of his shaft against her nether lips.

"You're ready for me," he said, relishing the dampness oozing from her interior. His hips levered forward a little as he sank an inch into her heated interior. She cried out again and crammed her hips down around him so he slid slickly into her.

Slocum stayed buried balls deep in her, relishing the tightness and warmth all around him. Looking down in her face made him wonder about the woman. How could Flora put up with all she had, work in shackles, then escape by climbing up half a mountain and be ready for this coupling?

Slocum groaned as she tightened all around him. He withdrew slowly, her inner muscles grasping at him the entire way. When only the head of his shaft remained within her, he paused, gathered his strength, and then sank back into her with a smooth movement. This rocked her back. Her knees came up on either side and then tightened so that her upper legs pressed into her breasts. He began stroking faster until she reached the point where she was clawing at his back and thrashing about under him.

"Oh, John, yes, don't stop. Don't, oh, don't!"

He was past the point of being able to stop. The heat all along his length burned down into his groin and set off a reaction he could not stop even if he had wanted. But he didn't. He thrust faster, grinding his crotch into hers. The slapping sounds were quickly drowned out by the woman's shrieks of pure sexual release.

As Flora cried out, her inner muscles clamped down hard on Slocum. He had reached the limits of his endurance. The hot tide rose within and then spilled out. For a moment the world went away for Slocum and then he came back to see a sweaty, flushed Flora looking up at him. She reached out, a shaky hand stroking his stubbled cheek.

"That was incredible, John. I never . . ." Her voice trailed off.

Slocum pushed up and away from her. Flora pulled down her skirt and then reached out for him. They lay together, arms around each other, but for Slocum, sleep was difficult to come by. Her soft, regular breathing gusted against his neck, but he strained to hear sounds of pursuit he knew had to be coming. If not now, then soon. Very soon.

17

"We're almost to the summit," Flora called to him. Slocum walked twenty yards behind her, constantly watching their back trail and peering down into the foggy pass for any sign that Galligan had ordered pursuit. It worried him that he saw nothing.

Whitey would have come after them on his own. Having two prisoners escape would have been an insult, but if he had told Galligan, there would have been a small army charging after them. Galligan could not lose. Ever. After the attack on his western gate and the way Slocum had so disheartened the guards on the wall, the emperor could never let him go.

Slocum considered the bodies tossed into the river and knew the howitzer had been doubly effective. Not only had it killed a lot of Galligan's gunmen, but it had also made the survivors less sure of the emperor's ability to protect them—or to make them rich off his wild-ass schemes.

"What a view!" Flora spun about, arms outstretched. Slocum looked up as her skirt flared and had to agree. Then

he brought up his rifle and almost fired. Two men grabbed
the woman and held her helpless between them.

He had a good shot at one but not the other. Flora blocked
the man hanging on to her right arm.

"Gotcha," crowed one.

Slocum got a good look at the other. Whitey. This time
he did snug the rifle to his shoulder and squeeze off a shot.
He cursed his eagerness to take out the white-haired old
man. His shot had gone wide by inches. Now all hell was
out for lunch.

Whitey dragged Flora back out of sight. Three of Galligan's henchmen whipped out their pistols and began firing,
in spite of Slocum being well protected by rocks along the
trail. He calmed himself and shot more accurately the second time. The gunman grunted and simply sat down. His
partners pulled him out of range, but Slocum knew he had
reduced the odds against him.

"We'll kill her 'less you surrender, Slocum!" Whitey
shoved Flora into the line of fire, but Slocum was already
moving. Being trapped on the narrow trail wasn't going to
get the woman free and would soon enough mean his own
death. Surrender to Whitey and get gunned down.

Climbing straight up a sheer rock face, Slocum moved
like a spider in his attempt to flank the men. He quickly
found himself thwarted by an outjut that he couldn't traverse.
Working laterally, he went farther from the trail head, hunting for the right spot to appear on the crest and open fire.

"Get him. Go on, get your asses down there and kill him!"
Whitey ranted and cursed when Slocum didn't cave in to his
demand for surrender.

Slocum fought to climb but found himself caught in a
dangerous situation. Below him was a hundred-foot drop.
The hand- and footholds on this rock face were few and far
between. He stretched and almost slipped. His rifle went
spinning down and seconds later came a report as the
weapon hit a rock and discharged.

The left handhold began to turn slippery with his own blood. Slocum wiped his hand off, balancing precariously to do so. But he gathered his strength, heaved, and found a better grip. He worked his way upward.

"He's dead, Whitey. Son of a bitch fell over the edge of the trail. That's his rifle way below."

"You see the body?"

"Fog's hidin' it."

"Go find it and drag it back to the lake."

A few more seconds passed as Slocum dangled from his rocky perch, but Whitey said nothing more. Muscles aching from strain, Slocum worked his way upward and finally flopped flat on the mountain ridge. Wiggling around, he pulled the six-shooter from his belt and looked around.

He was alone.

He got his feet under him and went hunting for Whitey. At the top of the trail he saw evidence where Whitey and his men had lain in wait, as if they knew exactly where their quarry would come up. Slocum looked along the ridge and realized that wasn't such a difficult guess to make. This was the only spot where anyone coming up from the pass could cross.

The trail down the western side of the mountain was steep. Slocum slipped and slid and then found a level area where several horses had been tethered. Whitey and his henchmen had ridden around to this point, hiked to the summit, and waited for their prey to walk right into their arms.

Slocum set off, thinking he might get a shot at Whitey and his men from one of the switchbacks. He was too late and never had the chance.

Flora was Galligan's prisoner again.

"Never seen a man eat like you, Slocum," Dr. Radley said. He tipped back the bottle of whiskey he had taken from his desk drawer but did not offer Slocum any. Slocum didn't want liquor. Water would do to wash down the second plate of food from the restaurant across the street. It wasn't particularly good, but Slocum had never tasted anything finer.

He belched, then said, "Galligan's not much on feeding his slaves."

"So he nabbed Flora Cooley again?" Radley shook his head.

"Last I saw him, Marshal Menniger was alive, though," Slocum said. "The deputies with him weren't as lucky."

"If you call bein' under Galligan's thumb lucky. Too bad about Hank, but least my nephew's still alive. Or was." Radley belched even louder than Slocum, then stuck the cork back in his bottle, looking longingly at the two fingers of amber liquid left inside. He tucked the bottle into his coat pocket for later. "I tried to get the cavalry to stir, but Galligan's paid them off too well."

"What about Bannock? He can't like the notion that the man who is selling him right of way is a kidnapper and murderer."

"You don't have much truck with railroad men, do you, Slocum? Truth is, Bannock don't much give two hoots and a holler how he gets through that pass. He sees a rail line over to Cheyenne and a spur down to Denver. For him that will mean a young fortune." Radley belched again. "Naw, not a young one, a huge one. Having the only railroad across the Grand Tetons and between the Northern Pacific and the spiderweb of 'roads through Denver, well, Bannock stands to be mighty rich."

"We have to strike again," Slocum said. "Quick, before Galligan can convince his ragtag army he has the upper hand. Saw how many of his men were killed by shrapnel from the howitzer barrage."

"Gonna be a hard sell. Even promisin' a bottle of whiskey each, it's gonna be hard gettin' men back."

"The man who was gun captain. What happened to him?"

"Dead. Now his assistant, Rafe, he spiked the cannon

and got away. Don't know if he's rarin' to go at Galligan again, but he might be."

"He looked to be a good artillerist, too," Slocum said. "A second attack matching the first one will break Galligan's hold on the pass."

Radley stroked his chin. "You oughta be talkin' to the men over at the saloon, not me."

"I'll leave that to you. I have to fetch the other howitzer."

"Won't be easy," Radley said, "but can't see fit to leave poor Hank up there. Nor Flora, for all that." Radley shot Slocum a gimlet stare. "She rubbed 'gainst you enough to make you think with your peter and not your head?"

"Does it matter? Galligan's got to be stopped if this town wants the railroad's bounty to flow to them rather than an outlaw."

Slocum thought of Flora and how they had parted. She had gotten him free, and the last night on the side of the mountain had been good, if exhausting. But as much as he owed her, he felt that he owed Beatrice just as much. More. She had sacrificed herself to decoy away Galligan's men. None of the attack against the western wall would have been possible without her bravery since no one in Thompson would have made the effort.

"Motives can be slippery as eels," Radley said, heaving to his feet. "You can find Rafe at the smithy's, if you want him to go with you. Might be he can scare up a few of his men to wrestle that there cannon down the hill again."

With that, Radley left.

Slocum polished off the rest of the gravy from his plate using the final crust of bread. He belched once more, leaned back, and thought about the job ahead of him. It was even more perilous an attack than before, since Galligan knew what he faced, and worse, knew what he had to lose if he didn't crush the town's spirit once and for all.

He left the doctor's office and headed toward the smithy's forge. He smelled hot metal and heard the slam of a hammer into hot iron long before he saw the small building set some distance from any other building. Whether Rafe had good sense to know what a tinderbox Thompson was or had built here and the rest of the town moved away from him, Slocum didn't know. From what he had seen of the man, Rafe had a good dose of common sense.

As Slocum entered, he squinted. Fumes rose from the open forge. Rafe looked up from the iron rod he had heated red hot.

"You still here, Slocum? Everyone said you hightailed it when the fighting got too hot." He slammed his hammer into the metal, flattening the rod into a flange. Two quick swings and a powerful twist bent the metal at right angles before getting tossed into a quenching bath.

Slocum waited for the loud hissing to die down before saying anything. He wanted to present his argument once, without interruption.

"A second attack will break Galligan," he said. "I got caught but escaped. The marshal's still alive, or was when I got away, and so is Flora Cooley." He couldn't tell what Rafe thought about that. The smithy turned away to hide his face. When he turned back, he had the right angle brace in his tongs again.

"You want me to help?"

"There's a second howitzer. We use it against the wall and Galligan loses most of his army."

"'Bout the way I see it, too." Rafe swung his hammer one last time, then tossed it onto his workbench. "He's gonna ruin my life if he keeps that wall up."

"How's that?"

"You ever know of a railroad that didn't need ironwork being done? Patching? Repairs? I can charge what I want unless Galligan is milkin' the 'road for all he can get pullin' on that teat. Cost too high in one place, they cut back everywhere else."

Slocum had to smile at this. It had never occurred to him

that anyone in Thompson would oppose Galligan over how many coins might jingle in his pocket.

"Let's go. Me and you can handle a single howitzer, if it's got a carriage as good as the other."

"Does," Slocum said. What he hadn't reckoned on was not wanting to remove the cannon.

Rafe scratched his chin as he stared at the howitzer. They had made good time up the hill to the mine, but Slocum had not counted on the smithy making such a pronouncement.

Rafe ran his hand along the cannon barrel and then stepped back.

"Ain't doin' us one bit of good. You put even a half charge in that howitzer and you'll be the one with shrapnel in your guts."

"There's a crack? I don't see it."

"Move closer. It ain't gonna bite you." Rafe held his miner's candle next to the brass barrel. He ran his broken fingernail along the smooth surface. Slocum saw it suddenly stop. The smith applied a little pressure and a good quarter inch disappeared into the metal.

"That's no magic trick, neither," Rafe said.

Slocum knelt and peered at the barrel, finally seeing what Rafe had right away. He couldn't tell how deep the crack ran into the metal and said so.

"You thinkin' I can patch it up?" Rafe shook his head. "Chances are good the crack doesn't go all the way through the barrel, but it doesn't have to. Weaken the metal, and when pressure from the gunpowder explosion pushes outward, there's no tellin' how the crack will spread."

"Might be good for one shot," Slocum said.

"Might be."

"But you wouldn't stand behind it?"

"Not even if you had a ten-yard-long lanyard on it. When a barrel blows up, it's elbows and assholes everywhere."

Slocum wondered if the mere sight of the howitzer set

up in front of the gate would spook the guards. They would be caught between fear of another barrage and Galligan behind them. He finally, reluctantly, decided that Galligan's drawn six-shooters would hold them in place more than the mere sight of a howitzer would run them off.

"Could we use it to blow up the gate?"

"Could," Rafe said, "but you might as well use just the gunpowder. Where the blast would go's more predictable."

Slocum leaned against the mine wall and felt the distant rumble of the underground river. He pictured the rushing river, the huge amount of water that had to pass through the mountain channel to feed the lake and produce such a swift current in what he'd dubbed Corpse River.

"Can we get the cannon onto its carriage?"

"More trouble than it's worth," Rafe said.

"I don't want to take it outside. I want to drag it deeper into the mine."

Rafe shrugged, wrapped his arms around it, and heaved.

"Don't weigh more 'n a hundred and fifty pounds," he said, grunting with the effort.

Slocum led the way to a spot where the rocky wall seeped water. He pointed to a spot at the base. Rafe dropped the howitzer.

"If that goes off there, you'll reduce the whole damn mine to rubble."

"Let's load it up. And bring all the powder."

Slocum started by laying a long trail of gunpowder from several yards away. When he reached the cannon, Rafe had finished loading it.

"I put in an extra charge, since you seem to want it to blow up. The shell will go smack into the wall." Rafe pressed his hand against the damp wall. "You thinkin' on bringin' a new source of water to town?"

"More like depriving Galligan of one." Slocum poured the rest of the powder in a huge mound in front of the muzzle, piled heavy rocks on top, and then backed off to check his handiwork. He had no idea what would happen, but he was sure as hell going to find out.

"Run for it," he advised Rafe. The smithy hesitated, then all Slocum heard were the heavy footfalls as the man raced from the mine.

Slocum went to the end of the line of gunpowder, flicked a lucifer, and recoiled a bit from its sulphurous flare. Then he dropped the match onto the end of the gunpowder. For a second he didn't think it would work, then the powder began to sizzle and pop. A small line of sparks crept away, following the gunpowder trail like an obedient ant.

"Confusion to my enemy!" Slocum cried.

Wasting no time, he followed Rafe from the mine shaft and burst out into the fresh clean air the instant the ground rumbled under his feet. A huge gust of wind from behind lifted him and sent him tumbling down the hill, a rain of rock debris and mud cascading over him.

As he lay facedown on the ground, he felt an even more powerful trembling.

"What the hell have you unleashed?" Rafe called.

Slocum didn't have any idea, but if it crashed down on Galligan, it had to be good.

18

Slocum expected to see a river flowing down the toll road through the ruptured gate on the wall. Instead all he saw was . . . nothing.

"Might be a trap," Rafe said. "Lure us closer, then spring up and take potshots at us at point-blank range."

"You think them varmints are that smart?" Doc Radley put a spy glass to his eye as he studied the wall for any sign of guards. He finally lowered it, shaking his head. "They're not that good. One of 'em would have popped up like a prairie dog to see what was going on. No movement a'tall."

The gate had been crudely repaired. A battering ram would knock it off its hinges, no howitzer required. What would be on the far side? Slocum envisioned Whitey, Gadsden, and a couple dozen of Galligan's cutthroats in hiding, waiting to open fire.

"I'll scout. You hang back until I give you the signal." Slocum dismounted and studied the terrain between the bend in the road where they had placed the howitzer before at the gate. The bed was in good shape, befitting a toll road. That might be another reason that Bannock was so eager to make a deal with Galligan. Half the work of leveling and widening had been done for railroad tracks. The train could be through the pass in weeks instead of months, and since summer was running down fast, the tracks could be on the far side of the pass and ready to cross the Wyoming plains before heavy snows fell. For all Slocum knew, Bannock might have crews already working westward from Cheyenne to meet tracks coming over the Grand Tetons.

That made it doubly to the railroad official's benefit to have a cooperative Galligan. What good would it be having tracks laid all the way to the mountains but nothing coming through the pass to connect with?

Slocum advanced cautiously, a new rifle clutched in his hand. He passed the spot where the armored wagon had tipped over and tumbled down the embankment into a ravine. Gus Cooley had been lucky once. Lady Luck had stopped smiling on him back in Thompson, thanks to Silas and his bank-robbing gang. But Hank Menniger was still on the other side of the wall.

Slocum wanted to find him alive. And Flora and Beatrice, too.

He reached the wall and peered up past the smooth stones, which reminded him of the ones he had been forced to load into Galligan's wagon. There wasn't any sign that the stones he had quarried had been used to repair the wall. A couple huge holes showed where the howitzer bombardment had taken its toll. Pressing close, he moved to the gate. Holes the size of his head had been blasted through the gate.

He put his eye to one hole and looked to the far side of the wall, hunting for any sign of movement. A rabbit ran across the road. Wind fitfully stirred vegetation that hadn't been cleaned off the roadway. But nowhere did he see any sign of guards.

Slocum used his rifle butt as a lever to pry open the gate far enough so he could slip through. Still wary, he moved from side to side hunting for Galligan's men. Only when he was sure they weren't standing guard on the wall but out of sight did he squeeze back through and wave on the posse to join him. It was considerably smaller than the men who had fought the first time, but with no resistance, Slocum hoped a dozen men would be enough.

Kill Galligan, destroy his empire. Those who followed him would fade away since there wouldn't be anything more to fight for.

"Come on. Nobody in sight," Slocum called. Radley and Rafe exchanged words, then passed the order along to the posse.

The riders rode as if they expected a dozen snipers to pop up. Slocum didn't blame them. He had the same feeling in his gut. Galligan had protected his domain too well for him to leave the wall unprotected. Yet his continued examination failed to turn up any sign of a trap.

The posse opened the gate farther and rode through. Slocum vaulted up into the saddle.

"Keep a sharp eye out for traps," he warned. Along this road he had run into guards waiting to take a potshot at anyone getting past the wall. But this time they rode to the edge of Top of the World before seeing anyone.

"What's happening?" asked Doc Radley. "Seen boomtowns empty like this, but Galligan wouldn't have let them go. No way would he give leave to even one man hightailin' it, not after Silas went after Lou's bank the way he did."

"Looks like a ghost town," Rafe said. "But I hear a roarin' noise. Where's it comin' from?"

Slocum looked at the uneasy posse. Lou Underwood had stayed in Thompson, to guard his bank, he said. With the mayor had gone the braver of the original attackers, leaving only those who were hunting for a few dollars promised by Radley. Slocum hadn't asked how much that was.

"There're some men, headin' south. And that's where the

noise is comin' from, 'less I miss my guess." Rafe pointed
to the motley band of riders leaving town, heading toward
the lake.

Slocum motioned for the posse to all go to the saloon.
He went in and looked around. The barkeep was packing
glasses in a box of excelsior. The man looked up, startled.
He blinked, then recognized Slocum and went for a weapon
hidden under the bar.

"If that's not an empty hand you bring back out, you're a
dead man." Slocum had his pistol out and aimed straight at
the bartender.

"Don't shoot, Slocum. Don't. I'm just—"

Slocum fired. The barkeep staggered back and dropped
the sawed-off shotgun he had tried to bring to bear. After
crashing into the back bar and breaking a considerable
amount of glassware, he slid to the floor.

"Bring him out here," Slocum said, the six-shooter remaining in his hand. He waited for Rafe and another posse
member to drag the barkeep out and drop him into a chair.
The man's white apron was decorated with a spreading red
blossom smack in the middle of his chest.

"You shot me," he said weakly. He looked up at Slocum
with accusing eyes.

"Where is everybody? Why were you packing up your
glasses? Going somewhere?"

"Lake," the barkeep gasped out. "Galligan's got everyone
stacking sandbags along the shore to keep the town from
bein' flooded. Huge hole opened up on the mountainside
where water's pourin' out. Don't know why. Just did."

"Flooded?" Doc Radley looked at Slocum. "Why's there
a flood now?"

"Nobody knows. Lake's risin' fast, too fast to drain out.
Water gushin' outta . . ."

Slocum laughed harshly. Detonating the howitzer in the
mine shaft had done what he had hoped, only not the way
he thought. Diverting the underground river had added to

the flowing waterfall, caused it to flood into the lake and threaten to wash Top of the World off the map.

"Is Galligan out there with the men working to save the town?" Slocum watched the barkeep closely. The man had turned white and his hand shook when he pressed it to his chest. He was dying fast. The flash of anger on the bartender's face gave Slocum what he thought might be the answer.

"Galligan's still in town," Doc Radley said, reading the expression the same way Slocum had. "He sent out the yahoos to save his town but he's not workin'. He's still here. You know where, Slocum?"

"The hotel. He uses that as his headquarters."

"What'll we do?" asked Rafe.

"Nuthin' to do 'bout this one," Radley said, pressing his fingertips into the man's throat. "He's deader 'n a doornail."

"Galligan's holding Deputy Cooley's wife prisoner. We got to rescue her. And he's likely to have the marshal, too. And others."

Radley looked sharply at Slocum, then nodded. He read more into what was said—and what wasn't—than most men. Slocum was glad he didn't have to play poker with the doctor. It was bad enough having Radley discern his motives as easily as he did.

"Are most of Galligan's men trying to keep the lake from overflowing?" Rafe asked. "This might be a sight easier 'n I thought."

"Time's against us," Slocum said. "Eventually they'll realize they can't plug the leak, and come back so they can leave town."

"We done better 'n I thought with that old howitzer. Never seen a barrel explode and cause such a commotion."

Slocum drew his six-shooter and checked to be sure he had six rounds in the cylinder.

"Rafe, you take some of them and circle from the left. Doc, take more and go right. Converge on the hotel."

"You intendin' to go it alone, Slocum?" Radley scowled. "That's not a good idea."

"Stop wasting time," Slocum said. He didn't let the doctor argue any more. If the posse closed in on both sides of the hotel, that would flush Galligan out. The emperor of Top of the World would have to come straight out into Slocum's gun sights.

He went directly to the hotel, walking slowly to give the others time to form the pincer attack. He wasn't surprised to see Whitey blocking the way. The old man had squared off and stood in the hotel door.

"You're damned near impossible to kill, Slocum. I sorta expected you when we couldn't find your carcass at the bottom of the mountain."

"How'd you know to go around and wait for us at the top?" Slocum asked.

Whitey laughed and it was ugly.

"You have a bad case of trustin' the wrong people," Whitey said. "You gonna talk me to death or you gonna draw?"

"I don't have a quarrel with you. I'm here for—"

"For Flora Cooley?" Whitey laughed again. "You are one dumb son of a bitch."

Slocum was already drawing as Whitey spoke, because he knew the old gunman wanted to distract him. Even with the small start, Slocum was almost too slow. Whitey might have been old but he was quick. But not as fast as John Slocum.

Whitey's six-gun was half out of his holster when Slocum's bullet tore through his chest, freezing him for an instant. Some reflex caused him to fire his pistol, in spite of still being in his holster. Slocum's second shot ended his life.

"You're even tougher than I thought, and that was mighty tough, indeed," came the mocking call. Slocum looked up. Galligan stood on the balcony running around the second story of the hotel. He had his six-shooter pressed into Flora's neck. "Drop the gun or I kill her." To emphasize his intent, Galligan cocked the six-gun and moved it to Flora's temple.

"You're not getting out of this alive, Galligan. Let her go and maybe I won't let the posse hang you like they did Silas."

"Silas," snarled the emperor. "Stupid of him to try to rob the bank. Me, I figured it all out how to rob the railroad and do it legally. They'll pay anything to put their tracks through the middle of my town."

"What'd you promise your men?" Slocum began shifting to his left to get a better shot at Galligan. Flora didn't move, silent and frightened in Galligan's grip. The outlaw's six-gun pressed hard into the side of her head.

"A steady income. They think Bannock will pay them each a hundred dollars every month."

"You're taking his money and clearing out," Slocum stated flatly.

"I knew it, I just knew it. You're not as stupid as you look, Slocum. What do I care about milking Bannock and his railroad for nickels every month? I want it so I can spend it."

"On whores?" Flora cried out, struggling for the first time. Galligan threw his left arm around her neck and bent her backward so she couldn't fight him.

"It won't matter to you, dear Flora. You're going to be dead, just like Slocum down there in the street."

Galligan jumped when the posse closed in on the hotel from both sides. Slocum wished they had hung back and let him deal with Galligan because the sight of the men made an already jittery Galligan even more nervous.

"I'm killing her, Slocum, then I'm killing you!"

Slocum raised his six-shooter and fired at the same time Galligan did. Slocum's heart skipped a beat because he knew he had missed. With his pistol shoved into Flora's temple, there was no way the emperor could have missed. But he had. Flora jerked away, spun, and crashed into the hotel wall.

Slocum started to fire again, but there was no need. Galligan took a step forward, his six-gun slid from nerveless fingers, and then he fell over the railing to the street.

Stepping out from a doorway came Beatrice, a smoking pistol in her hand.

She peered down at the dead outlaw and then dropped her gun.

"Slocum, Slocum!"

The cry tore his attention away from the two women on the balcony to where Rafe pointed.

"We got company!"

"All of Galligan's men. Every last one of 'em headin' our way!" corrected Doc Radley.

Slocum turned to face the onslaught. All he saw was a solid wall of mounted men charging hard at him, whooping and hollering as they came. He lifted his six-shooter, intending to take as many with him as he could before they killed him.

19

"Take cover!" Beatrice yelled from above. "They'll ride you down!"

Slocum aimed his gun, then decided the red-haired woman was right. Standing in the middle of the street was suicidal—just like facing scores of outlaws. He barely reached the boardwalk when the first of the riders flashed past.

To his surprise, they never slowed, and not one of the riders reached for his six-shooter. All they wanted was to ride away.

"What's goin' on?" Doc Radley asked, clutching his six-gun tightly. "Where are they goin' in such an all-fired hurry?"

"Look, that's Marshal Menniger!" Rafe made his way to the middle of the street when the last of Galligan's men had ridden past. "Marshal! We come to rescue you!"

Slocum didn't see that Hank Menniger needed any rescuing. The man rode a horse with the rest of the outlaws. It was almost as if he was chasing them, but that was ridiculous. How could a lone rider stampede dozens of armed gunmen?

"Get out of here," the marshal cried. "Get out now!"

Slocum stepped out and saw water sloshing along the main street of town. Then the water turned into a wall. And the wall turned into an outright flood.

The first few inches lapped at his ankles, but the power of the water spun him around and sent him staggering. He got back to the boardwalk and stepped over Whitey as water began thundering along. Galligan's body was swept up and carried off, to vanish in white froth within yards. And the water kept rising.

"The whole damn lake's overflowing," Menniger cried. "They tried to stop it with sandbags but there's too much to stop. Too damned much!" And then he was gone, trying to outrun the rapidly rising water.

"John!"

He couldn't tell which woman called to him. With the water chasing him into the hotel lobby, he took the steep steps to the second floor three at a time and burst out into the corridor. He found the door leading to the balcony where Flora and Beatrice stood staring at the flood below.

"What's happening?" Flora asked.

"Doesn't matter," Slocum said, not wanting to own up to his part in causing the catastrophe. He turned to Beatrice and stared into her bright green eyes. "Thanks for taking care of Galligan."

"I wish I could have done it earlier. Lots earlier."

Before Slocum could say a word, the hotel shifted under them. Slocum found himself with his arms around both women. Under other circumstances, it would have been pleasurable, even memorable, having to decide which to kiss first. Now the trio was buffeted about. He felt like a flea on a hot griddle as the hotel began twisting first one way and then the other.

The flood waters rose precipitously and tore off part of the railing.

"The whole hotel's going," Flora cried. "Save me, John. Save me!"

Slocum grabbed for Beatrice as she tottered and almost fell into the water only a foot below the balcony now. He swung her around so she could get her footing.

"Leave the bitch! Save *me*!" Flora screeched and ran at Beatrice. She shoved her into the raging current. "We can be rich, John. Me and you. Gus was nothing. He wouldn't run for mayor, but you got ambition. I know it. We can be rich if we work Bannock for what he was going to give Galligan."

She clung to him.

"Save me. We can be rich and—"

Slocum shoved her from him, grabbed a long piece of the wooden railing, and plunged into the torrent. Even with the added buoyancy of the wood, he was pulled under and thought his lungs would explode before he popped to the raging surface. A flash of red hair a dozen yards away showed where Beatrice fought the water.

He kicked and tried to steer himself toward her. She struggled feebly now, exhausted by the supreme power of the water.

"Don't give up, Beatrice!" he shouted.

"Never," came the weak reply. "Not after all I been through . . ."

She disappeared underwater. Slocum kicked powerfully, letting the current take him toward her—or where she had been. Abandoning his railing, he dived into the roiling water. Twisted and turned in all directions by the current, he fought downward until he saw the telltale red mop of hair again. He grabbed. He caught some of it and pulled. Beatrice fought him, showing she was still alive.

He got his arms around her body again as they popped to the surface like corks, and then Slocum cried out as he smashed into a rock. Beatrice slipped from his grip. Fighting for his own life, he succeeded in bouncing off another large rock and then rounding it to find a more tranquil pool in the river. He thrashed about, got his feet under him, and finally reached the riverbank.

It took a few seconds for him to realize they had been washed through town and had somehow ended up in the river pouring down the eastern slope. He saw a body bob about and vanish.

Corpse River.

"Beatrice!" He cried for her again but heard nothing except the roar of rushing water. Stumbling along the riverbank, he continued heading downslope hunting for her.

Again her red hair proved the beacon. He saw her clutching a tree limb as the river tossed her about. Running hard now, he reached a bend in the river where he could dive in ahead of her and let the river bring the woman to him. They tumbled over and over in the water and finally found themselves washed up on the riverbank.

Slocum tried to tend her but all he could do was cough up water. Beatrice finally came to him.

"Some rescuer you are. You didn't even ask how I am."

"Figured you'd come out just fine. You always do, don't you?" Slocum looked up into her bright eyes. She looked like a drowned rat. Her clothing had been partially ripped away and her hair now hung in filthy curtains around her face. He brushed it back.

"Looks like I have again," she said.

"Yeah," Slocum said, kissing her.

Beatrice pushed back from him and asked, "You going back for that other woman?"

He thought for a moment, then said, "What other woman?"

This time they had plenty of time for the kiss.

Watch for

SLOCUM AND THE SOCORRO SALOON SIRENS

392nd novel in the exciting SLOCUM series
from Jove

Coming in October!

DON'T MISS A YEAR OF

Slocum Giant
by
Jake Logan

penguin.com/actionwesterns

OCT 1 8 2011